Tales of
Unkosher Souls

Tales of
Unkosher Souls

David Margolis

gatekeeper press™

Columbus, Ohio

Tales of Unkosher Souls

Published by Gatekeeper Press
2167 Stringtown Rd, Suite 109
Columbus, OH 43123-2989
www.GatekeeperPress.com

The editorial work for this book is entirely the product of the author. Gatekeeper Press did not participate in and is not responsible for any aspect of this element.

Library of Congress Control Number: 2021937367

ISBN (paperback): 9780991215478
eISBN: 9780991215461

Contents

Introduction

How does a poorly observant Jew, suddenly get the chutzpah to write about his fellow Jews? It wasn't easy, but writing about anything isn't easy, even composing a grocery list can be a challenge for a septuagenarian like myself. Some of the characters in this book live in shtetls—Jewish villages in czarist Russia—and some in the modern era, except for the dinosaur that lives in the Garden of Eden and the boulder that lives by the seashore. Somewhere in the midst of my writing, I realized that I'm one of a dwindling group of people who actually knew someone who grew up in a shtetl. My grandparents, Laika and Pinya Margolis, immigrated to Winnipeg, Canada from Olgopol, a small village in Russia, in 1906. My grandfather was a very funny man who spoke somewhat broken English, and although he's been dead for fifty years, his speech and humor are present in many of the subjects that appear in this very short book.

I conceived *Tales of Unkosher Souls* after I enrolled in a St. Louis adult education course given by Howard Schwartz, a scholar of Jewish mysticism and mythology.

I became fascinated by the Hasidic tales that we read. Stories about dybbuks and golems, and souls that transmigrated into animals, plants and even rocks. There were narratives about legendary rabbis with supernatural powers, and anecdotes about the Jewish Messiah soon to appear on this earth, all the while attempting to explain how humans came to be, why we exist, and our ultimate destination after we die. Many of the characters are hatched from these Hasidic stories except that the religious people are replaced by impious doubters and sinners. Yet, when misfortune befalls them, most have a desire to believe in a god, if only they could. I include myself in that category.

Call Me Stein

I celebrated a birthday last Tuesday. It's been exactly two billion years since a volcano disgorged me from the earth's belly, and that's old, even for a rock. I was a brute back then, black obsidian, and the size of a boxcar with sharp edges. The last thing you'd want to do was clamber over me with a thin-skinned hide. Over time, the wind, the rain, the hurricanes, and the snowstorms left their mark, and after more than an eon, I'd shrunk to the size of a refrigerator. Slowly, and I mean excruciatingly slowly, the cool breezes stopped, while the humid atmosphere produced rains every day of the year. A sea formed. Fish appeared and sea gulls swooped down from out of the blue for their daily ration of seafood. Waves lapped against me and wore off one side more than the other, so that I became a black shiny boulder with an eccentric hump and a greenish streak of chromium. This was so unusual that I came to believe I wasn't meant to be a rock, maybe I was meant to be something else, a leech or a snail or a turtle with a black shell. But maybe not, I hadn't moved for twenty thousand years, since the last earthquake, and no turtle's that slow.

Around a hundred million years ago, it seems like just yesterday, a large bird landed on me. It was black and shiny, too. Of course, birds had perched on me before, but this one was different. "How dee do," it said in a language that I instantly understood. The fowl squirted some excrement on my lumpy hump, and it rolled down my left side. "The name is Duddy," the bird announced.

"Call me Stein," I said, although I'd never been called that. In fact, I'd never been called anything by anyone in all the years of my existence.

"You know, you're one hell of a rock, one hell of a dazzling rock, a rock with a bump, I had my eye on you for a long time."

"I don't think I've ever seen you before."

"Remember that eel that slithered around and around you, and that black bass that nibbled some algae growing at your base? That was me in disguise, checking you out."

"And?"

"And you might just be perfect for us."

"Us?"

"Yeah us. You may not know it, but you've got something inside you, and not every rock can boast something like that."

"Something like what?"

"Something special. Something that was put there when the earth belched and catapulted you into the world."

"Someone put something in some part of me? But who could that somebody be?"

"Someone with an overall plan for all of the heavens and the oceans and the moons and the stars and the sun."

"But not you?"

"No, not me, I'm just a messenger, I like to think of myself as a facilitator."

"So, who is it?"

"Let's just call him *The Supreme Mensch*."

"And what does this almighty mensch want with me?"

"He plans to create some other creatures, smarter than stones or rocks or even birds for that matter. He'll want them to have something too, so your something might really be something sometime."

～

A few epochs went by. Nothing. Oh sure, lots of crows and gulls rested on me, a few storks, and even an albatross or two, but not Duddy. Fish came by, but fish don't talk; they've got a tough enough time breathing through their gills, never mind talking. Salamanders darted here and there, and some eels shot me a few volts. I figured they might be my bird friend in disguise, checking me out, but there was no proof. Your imagination can play tricks when you're immobile. I began to despair, because when someone tells a boulder that you could be something, of course you jump at it. Ask any butte or even a pebble, they'd all tell you the same thing. What's the point of millions of years of existence, if you're sitting half covered in water?

The bird finally returned. "Hey, Stein, how's it hangin'?" Then it laughed like it was a joke, some joke.

"Where you been, Duddy? I've been waiting."

"I got orders to move you. You see, there's this beautiful place with trees and flowers and fruit and all, and there's some creatures living there that have an essence inside, like you. Yahweh thought it might be a good place for you to exist."

"*Yahweh?*"

"Yeah, that's his name now, The Supreme Mensch is now *Yahweh.*"

"Sure, that'd be fine, anything's better than existing here."

Right then, the raven grabbed me with his talons-- I'd eroded down to the size of a paving stone--and we climbed high in the sky. I could feel the wind rolling over me and under me, with sunshine glinting off the lumpity bump on my back. We flew over an ocean and a continent until Duddy swooped low and dropped me into a stony path, between some igneous chaps and a feldspar. "I'll be back soon to see if you're adjusting," the bird hollered out as it flew away. The bird was right. There were lots of things that I'd never seen: daffodils and dahlias, pines and oaks with needles and leaves, noisy parrots, blue whirring hummingbirds, and rabbits galore, soft stuff, not a slab like me.

Early the next morning, a naked figure walked by on two legs. Its feet massaged my excrescence as it walked over me. The creature was soft and round with long golden hair tied in the back, the same color as the moss that grew between its legs. The skin was perfect and white, the eyes soft and blue, not stiff like a fish, with a beguiling smile that beguiled me. I quivered with desire, if a stone can ever be said to have desire, or even quiver. I figured it might come along this road for the next thousand years, plenty of time for me to make my move.

Duddy showed up a few days later. "Well Stein, I guess there's some better sights here, than at the seashore."

"Sure is. That two-legged gem made my obsidian obscene."

"Eve?"

"That its name?"

"*Her* name, she's a *she, a woman,* not an it. You're an *it,* a rock's an *it.* Yahweh created her."

"Perhaps you brought me here to be her companion?" I queried timorously.

"Sorry Stein, Yahweh's already made someone for her, *a man,* a *he.* His name is Adam. I'm surprised you haven't run in to him."

"But Adam could mess up, and I'd be Plan B."

"Possibly, but I'm just a messenger, a fowl messenger," Duddy twittered.

The next day, Eve came by. She was accompanied by a gawking gangly fellow with a hose and a couple of balls in a sack. I guessed it was Adam. He laughed with an annoying hee-haw, and his teeth were stained yellow. He surely wasn't much, but then maybe I was jealous, he being my rival. A greasy snake slithered up to them, and they all whispered amongst each other as they climbed a tree and ate some apples. After that, they joined together.

The next day, all hell broke loose. A fierce tornado arose from the heavens, and the flowers, the trees, and the animals were caught up in the huge vortex. I rolled down the road, and ended up in a deep dark ravine as the garden disappeared into the firmament. I wedged between some large granites as water rushed over me. Then all was still.

I must have been a century or two in the gorge. The water had diminished to a trickle when I spotted Duddy, flapping his gaping wings, negotiating through the small opening in the earth's surface. Even before landing, the feathered emissary was making excuses.

"It didn't work out," Duddy said.

"I presumed that."

"They didn't obey Yahweh's commands, and they reveled in their lasciviousness."

"Oh?"

"Yahweh had to blow the whole thing away, it's kaput."

"I wouldn't have done anything like whatever they did. I would have loved her. She could have stood on me for an eternity."

"What's done is done. Yahweh told me to fly you back to the seashore."

"If Yahweh wouldn't mind, I'd like to stay here. It's quite cozy in the bottom of the canyon."

"Stein, I'll be frank. I don't think this is the time to bother Him about something as insignificant as yourself. I can put in a good word for you sometime in the future, but not now." The bird gathered me up, and we flew over the continent and the ocean. Then it dropped me back by the water's edge.

The climate became frigid and the sea dried up. It snowed almost forever, before a huge glacier rolled over me. Nine hundred thousand years later, a stronger sun provided heat, melting the ice and leaving a vast field of stones including myself. Shoots of greenery came up, forming meadows of tall weaving grass, almost as bucolic as the garden that blew away.

And one day I saw a man. He talked and walked like Adam, but he was wearing a red shirt and blue overalls. There was a beautiful woman, with two children, and soon there were six, and I knew that Yahweh was back on the job. They grew corn and wheat and they prospered, but a century or two later, some big machines dug holes for foundations that destroyed the crops. Houses were built followed by fire stations, libraries, schools and parks. I saw children grow up, get married and have their own children who then had children.

I was lucky or maybe it was fate. I was placed in a park along the edge of a trail, just as most of my buddies were ground up and put in a cement mixer to become a road or a building. The houses were eventually torn down, office buildings sprang up and trains groaned underground, but they kept the park and the path where I sat.

Duddy stopped by one day. "Well whaddya think?"

"Think?"

"Civilization man, civilization. Look at that church over there with that steeple and the bell chiming every hour. That's where they worship the Father, the Son and the Holy Ghost."

"That many?"

"The Father, the Son, the Ghost, Yahweh, Supreme Mensch, it's all the same, different words for God."

"What about the… the something that you said *I* had?"

"You still got it. That's how I found you again."

"I dream of Eve. Any chance she might come by sometime?"

"Sure, sometime, Stein."

The climate changed, it became warmer and stopped snowing. Icebergs melted, and oceans swelled, scientists said that Man had caused it. One day, the seawater broke through the dikes and inundated the city, drowning the people. After a few centuries, the vacant buildings crumbled and tumbled into the sea. I fell to the bottom and lived with the dead fish and the dead whales and the dead humans. The planet cooled again and the ice came and went, and came and went.

⌐

Now, I'm back on the seashore with water lapping against my sides. I've lost my hump and my streak, and I'm the size of a lump of charcoal.

The bird came back this morning. "How dee doo Stein, happy birthday."

"Thanks, Duddy. I'd offer you some birthday cake if I had any. Too bad about civilization, eh." I couldn't resist a dig after the false hopes I'd received from this carnival chirper.

"Things didn't work out like they were supposed to." The bird looked down at its claws.

"You ever see Big Mensch?" I asked.

"You bet, He's still talking about the future. He's preserved all the somethings from the humans He created. When the conditions are right, He'll be bringing some of them back and getting things humming again."

"Those toes and that arch, I'll never forget her."

"Yeah, your essence came that close," Duddy placed his wings about two inches apart, "from making a pizazz in paradise."

"But what about now, what will happen to me now? I've been waiting so long, this being my two billion and first year."

"He mentioned you the other day, that's why I'm here."

"He did? He really did? No kidding?"

"No kidding. He's got a plan for you."

"A plan, my gosh, finally a plan."

"You'll be a witness to it all."

Moshko's Lovers

Moshko Mandelshtam was an unhandsome endomorph. He was short in stature, and short in the arms with a bit of a paunch, not to mention a disconcerting wart at the tip of his reddish nose. He worked as a shoemaker in his Uncle Heschel's business, sewing the tongue into the vamp of the shoe. On a good day, Moshko was able to secure about fifty tongues, and Heschel boasted that his nephew was the most industrious worker in the shtetl, especially when compared to his own two sons, Shmuel and Dovidl, who were on the lazy side of the work ethic, playing their Klezmer music in the taverns along the bustling main street of Posukeva, or at least it had once bustled, before the railroad passed it by, and before strikes, pogroms, and devastating fires took their toll.

Moshko supported himself and his mother, Luba, with his modest wage, and she helped out by peddling her hand-knitted shawls and blankets in the Posukeva marketplace and at the annual fairs in the larger towns of Tulchin and Nemirov. His father, may he rest in peace, had died when Moshko was only three. He'd been thrown from his wagon by a spooked team of horses while transporting a load of vodka, and there were scandalous rumors of his father tippling the brew just before the accident occurred. Luba never remarried, preferring to cherish the fond memories of her dear Nachum.

Moshko would arrive home around seven in the evening, and after a repast of herring with onions and sour cream and a bowl of soup with kreplach, he would fall like a log into his bed for the night. Yet, this was the time for the action to begin, for Moshko Mandelshtam was a dreamer. He would dream about the love of a woman, normal for a young man just turned twenty-one, but other times he dreamed of his soul, and the beings it had inhabited before inserting inside himself, and sometimes the soul and the love would blend together.

According to Jewish lore, his spirit was minted in the Tree of Souls at the time when God created the world. After residing in a blossom, on a twig, on a branch, Moshko's soul was plucked by the Angel Gabriel and placed in the body of a lamb. But this was no ordinary ungulate, it was tended by the Patriarch Jacob when he worked for his uncle Laban, and it travelled with Jacob to the land of Canaan. After the sheep died, the soul was allocated to some goats and even a haughty rooster, before entering an Israelite slave who followed Moses out of Egypt. Over the centuries, it had known a Greek philosopher, a courtier to Henry the VIII, a walrus hunter, and a Maasai warrior in Kenya.

Moshko's soul was kind and sensible, even if the angel had never assigned it to a famous personage, unless one considered a ewe from the bible to be noteworthy. Most of the reincarnations were a bit stubby like Moshko, but they were all devoted to their children and their intelligent, funny, sensuous, dark-eyed wives, except, of course, for the time it spent inside a chicken. Some of the dreams encompassed an entire night, and were interrupted only by the sun's rays peeking through a crack in the curtains of his room.

Occasionally, his fantasy would transform to a nightmare, as when husband and wife grew tired of Moses' dithering on the top of the mountain, and Korah enticed them to worship the golden calf. Their souls were sent to Gehenna (Jewish Hell) and endured interminable punishments. Moshko would awake, drenched in sweat, after a dream like that.

ᔈ

One day, Heschel approached the young man as he was putting the fortieth tongue in the twentieth pair of shoes. "I've been talking to your mother, Moshko, it's time that you married."

"Married?" No one including his mother had ever mentioned such a prospect, and when you're a shy, unattractive shoemaker, there isn't much in the way of opportunity. The dark-eyed beauty of his dreams was just that, in his dreams.

"And we have the perfect woman for you. She's anxious to meet a silver-tongued shoemaker like yourself." Heschel laughed at his jocosity.

"Who might she be?"

"Why Hanna, Simon Averbuch's daughter. We've even talked about merging our shoemaking businesses."

"Hanna? The woman who is divorcing Israel Kornblum after he had an affair with the bar-maid in Skivapolie?"

"Yes, that's the one. Simon was grooming Israel to take over the business, then boom, he's moved to Cleveland Ohio. Hanna is cheery, she bakes a beautiful bread, and a soup you could die for."

"You know that for sure, that you've eaten her soup and you're ready to die if you don't get more?"

"No, but I've heard about it. They say she's a good cook, and she's tall and stately, maybe a little fleshy under the arms and generous in the tuchus, but with such a complexion, free of pimples and—"

"Fat like me?"

"Maybe a bit plumpish, but you two would make a good fit. Luba and I ran it past Rabbi Perl. He says it's a marriage made in heaven. He'll push for the divorce as soon as possible, but you need to go see her today before—"

"Before what?"

"Before she's snapped up by Menachem Felch, the potato farmer. There's a rumor that he's visited her more than once and brought with him some of the best golden tubers in all of the fields around Posukeva, but surely, she wouldn't turn down a successful shoemaker for a potato grower?"

That very evening, as instructed by his uncle, Moshko took a bath and put on his only suit with a new white shirt and a high starched collar. After undergoing a shave from the best barber in the Posukeva, he knocked on Hannah's door and stood up as straight as he could. She was a tall woman, finely dressed, and wearing a special perfume for the occasion. As Moshko sniffed her intoxicating scent and examined the smooth skin of her chubby white hands, he began to believe that this was his lucky day, but when he looked up into her face, his hopes fell, for her eyes were squinted, her ear lobes displayed an unnatural deep crimson, and her full lips had thinned to a scowl. "I was expecting someone else," she said.

"You were expecting a man of the earth?"

"Yes, I was expecting Menachem, the potato producer. We're getting married as soon as my *get* is signed by the rabbi."

"But my uncle led me to believe that you hadn't made a final decision, and that you might be interested in marrying a successful cobbler, a kind and sensible man, who would be devoted to you and our children."

She gazed down at him, scrutinizing his scrubbed countenance, then honed in on the wart at the tip of his nose. "I've already decided, and it's not you."

Moshko went back to sewing tongues and dreaming, but Heschel hadn't given up. He'd recently been to Nemirov on business, and while there, he'd heard that a rabbi was looking for just the right husband for his daughter. Heschel's heart swelled, believing that his exemplary nephew would be the perfect fit for a religious man's daughter. It wasn't more than three days until the bathed and suited Moshko Mandelshtam was greeted by Mindel Zipursky at the door of her spare bungalow. Moshko noticed that she was thin and bony with a wandering eye, but then, how did a short fat man such as himself, appear to her?

"Well, you must be Mothko," she said with a slight lisp. Moshko thought to himself, *so she speaks with a lisp, there's worse things in the world than a speech impediment.* She indicated that he should come in, and they sat down on the settee in the unpretentious parlor.

"Yes, I've come from Posukeva, I rose very early and travelled six hours in a donkey cart just to see you." He smiled sweetly, and no one could doubt that this was a kind-hearted man.

"And so, you must have risen even earlier to put on your tallis and tefillin to say your morning prayers."

"I must tell you. I work very hard in the shoe factory, and we start almost at the crack of dawn, such that it's very difficult to say the morning blessings most days."

"And so, you must then have time for the afternoon prayers and then the evening prayers?"

"Well yes, sometimes, if I'm not too tired. But I want you to know that I'm a successful cobbler, a worthy and honest man, who would be devoted to you and our children."

Mindel seemed troubled. "So then, you're not religious with your clean-shaven face."

"Yes I am. In fact, God has allowed me to know all the people in history who have shared my soul. He has given me special powers." Moshko smiled broadly and Mindel brightened.

"Tell me about some of those people, Mothko." Just then, the door from the kitchen opened, and the prospective bride's parents appeared with smiles of encouragement on their faces. At the same time, the redolence of a delicious baked chicken wafted toward Moshko's nostrils, and he imagined that Mindel would be an excellent cook if she was half as accomplished as her mother.

"I remember being in the court of Henry VIII during the great feast of St. Stephen. He was on his fifth wife then or maybe his fourth, and the cooks roasted her favorite meal, suckling pig. The animal came sizzling off the spit, and we carried it in on a huge platter just as Catherine and Henry sat down to eat. In no time, the ravenous Henry…"

"You ate *treif*?" In his enthusiasm, Moshko realized that he'd made a mistake. Rabbi Zipursky appeared mortally wounded, although his wife still appeared hopeful. Mindel frowned, and her delicate complexion turned even paler.

"Well, no, I generally ate the ducks and the geese if they were available…"

"But they couldn't have been killed in the kosher style?" Mindel's voice started to rise.

"Well, I wasn't a Jew then. My soul doesn't have a choice where it goes. But can I tell you about the time that my spirit inhabited Jacob's sheep? Yes, *the* Jacob, from the bible. My tenderloins and chops were delicious and as kosher as a torah scroll!"

Moshko spent the night at the inn in Nemirov, where he was lucky to get the last bowl of turnip stew to quell his hunger. He washed it down with a large glass of vodka, and he dreamt that night of the aforementioned lamb, munching grass in the pastoral pasture.

﹌

Six months later, Heschel received a letter from a childhood friend, Dr. Hyman Slovpinksy, who had lived in Kiev for many years. It turned out that Dr. Slovpinsky had four daughters, all one year apart, and even a man with the stature of a physician had difficulty coming up with husbands for all of them. He was seeking a partner for his youngest daughter, Shaina, and was hoping that Shmuel or Dovidl might still be available. However, against their father's expressed wishes, Shmuel had moved to Nemirov with his Klezmer band, and Dovidl had joined him there, playing the clarinet and bartending part time. Heschel wrote back that his sons were unavailable, but his nephew, Moshko Mandelshtam, was looking for a wife, and Shaina would be well-served marrying a young man of his caliber. He invited the Slovpinskys for a Shabbat dinner, to be specially prepared by his wife, Malka, and Moshko's mother, Luba.

On the appointed evening, the prospective bride-to-be and her father were several hours late. The soup had gone cold and the brisket had dried out, with the potatoes congealing into a lumpy mass, engulfing the carrots and parsnips in the conglomerate. Luba and Malka buzzed around nervously, watching their dinner slowly disintegrate, while Heschel stoically drank his vodka. Moshko perspired copiously, soaking through his freshly ironed shirt.

Finally, there was a knock on the door, and a well-dressed young woman entered. Moshko got up from his chair to enunciate a greeting, but his throat went dry and mute when he saw her penetrating dark eyes and perfect teeth, like in his dreams. She was followed by Dr. Slovpinksy in a well-fitted blue suit, carefully trimmed moustache, and marvelous silver hair combed straight back. Heschel smiled broadly as the men embraced, patting each other on the back several times. Moshko shook the doctor's hand, embarrassed that he hadn't brought a handkerchief to dry his sweaty palms.

"It's been such a long time, doctor. It's a great honor for you and your daughter to come visit with us," said Malka.

"I'm sorry we're late, the train to Tulchin broke down. And please don't call me doctor, dearest Malka. I prefer Hyman or better yet, Hymie. That's what they called me growing up in Posukeva, and that's what my wife still calls me along with some other names that I won't mention." He laughed, and Heschel guffawed a little too loudly.

"Too bad Rochel couldn't come," said Malka.

"We've got a wedding for daughter number three in two weeks, and she's got her hands full, but I promised Shaina a trip to Berlin to hear the opera, and of course, a visit here to see old friends." Then they all sat down to the dinner table.

"Heschel, it seems like yesterday that we were playing in mud puddles on this very street," remarked Hymie with a broad grin.

"You were quite the little devil as a young pup, stealing apples and pears and even some cookies from the vendor carts," said Heschel, and they laughed again, as if stealing was something to laugh about.

"And we never got caught, did we?" The two men giggled some more, caught up in their love for one another, as they recalled the unpunished waywardness of their boyhoods.

"And Moshko, your dad was with us too," said Hymie. Moshko nodded his head. What could he say to that?

"Nachum always spoke so highly of you," said Luba.

"And just think, that naughty little boy, stealing and skipping school, turned out to be the greatest ear, nose and throat specialist in all of Russia. Looking at him now, you wouldn't believe what an imp he was," added Heschel reverently.

"Enough, enough," said Hymie. "Let's get the blessings over with so we can drink some wine. I know that my dear friend here, has a good bottle for me." He snickered again, and Heschel howled like he'd heard a joke.

"And the time when we skipped Hebrew school and went swimming in the pond at the end of the street, and those girls from the nun's school were there too. After dark, I took some vodka from Papa's cellar…" They went on and on, each tale taller and racier than the next.

They said the prayers, lit the candles, drank the wine and ate the bread. They started on the fish appetizer, and moved on to the reheated brisket with revitalizing gravy, as Hymie and Heschel continued with their bragging and bantering and foolish jocularity. The smiles from Luba and Malka remained fixed, Moshko fretted and sweated, and Shaina looked bored.

After dinner, the guests were served Sumatra coffee and Turkish figs, and the men downed shots of whiskey before devouring several pieces of Malka's honey cake.

Finally, Shaina spoke up. The old people hushed, surprised to hear her voice.

"I met your sons, Shmuel and Dovidl, a few nights ago in Kiev. Their band was playing in a tavern, and I got up and sang with them. We started talking and I realized that they were from Posukeva. Shmuel conducts the band, and Dovidl is a brilliant clarinet player. They want me to sing at a wedding next month, you should come and hear them play."

Heschel lost the mirth in his eyes. "I'm not speaking to my sons. They left without my permission, and we're still looking for workmen to replace them." Then he nodded toward Moshko and brightened again, "But no one can make shoes like Moshko here, no one works as hard as this boy, and he fixes all our equipment too."

"And what else do you do Moshko, outside of work?" inquired Shaina. Moshko's red face turned a deeper shade, as her bright eyes fixed on him.

"I work ten hours in the shoe factory, every day except the Sabbath, so I don't have time for hobbies." Moshko stared down at his plate. He didn't think a woman of her caliber would be interested in hearing about his honesty, or his soul and its incarnations, or about anything else that he had to say.

"He tinkers with the lathe and the polisher, and he sews all the tongues, he even creates patterns for the new styles," commented Heschel. "When I retire, I'm hoping that he'll take over the business, if we still have a business after the imports from Hungary and Vienna take all of our customers. He'll make a great husband, too."

"Well, do you have a wife in mind?" asked Shaina.

"Your father and I exchanged letters for two months, and we thought it would be you," interjected a surprised Heschel before Moshko could answer.

"What are you talking about?" Now it was Shaina's turn to blush.

"Heschel and I thought if you just came and met the lad, you might allow him to court you, and he in turn would ask for your hand in marriage," said the doctor rather stiffly.

"You told me we were going on a trip to your boyhood home, and then we'd take the train to Berlin, and we'd inquire about my singing lessons with Herr Deichmann. You didn't mention getting married, and you didn't tell me that I'd have to sit and listen to your stupid stories about your boyhood pranks." Her eyes flashed with anger, as her dark curls bounced up and down. This wasn't a woman who would put up with such a feckless father, even if he was a doctor.

"I just wanted you to meet a perfectly good man from a good family, and if you met him and liked him, you might lose those ridiculous ideas of a woman singing in a band. Instead you open such a foul mouth to me!"

"He just sits there, staring at his plate as if he might find a wife there, and suddenly I'm supposed to marry him?" Shaina pointed her finger at poor Moshko, as a drop of sweat rolled off the wart on his nose and onto the dessert plate. "And my own father raises his voice to me in front of people that I've never met!" Shaina got up from the table, walked to the front door, opened it, then slammed it behind her.

"Should we go after her?" asked a distressed Luba.

"No, she'll find her way to the inn. She's very resourceful."

"Would you care for some brandy? We can drink it out on the porch and smoke some Virginia cigars," said Heschel.

"A perfect way to end the evening," said Hymie, as if nothing had happened.

⁓

After Moshko recovered from his humiliation, he realized that Shaina had every right to be angry with her father. Their generation was starting to think for themselves, seeking jobs with better pay and working conditions, and finding spouses on their own. Why not join a band if that's what you wanted to do? He wrote to Israel Kornblum inquiring about a job in Cleveland; he replied that there was always an opening for a good worker.

And so, Moshko packed his bags, bought a train ticket to Hamburg, a third-class passage to New York, and another train ticket to Cleveland. He began work at the Steinhart Shoe Company, and soon rose to foreman, and then to supervisor in the maintenance division, repairing the sewing machines, and installing equipment that ran on the newly invented electricity. He patented a device that would mechanically sew the tongues to the vamps, tripling the number of shoes that could be produced each day. Mr. Steinhart promoted him to vice-president as the company opened one factory after another.

∽

Six years later, Moshko Mandelshtam returned to the shtetl after receiving notification that his Uncle Heschel had passed away. He planned to settle his mother's affairs and take her back to the United States. Luba greeted him at the train station in Tulchin.

She scrutinized him after they kissed. "You've changed Moshko, you look so different, like a man, not a boy." Moshko was just as short, and the wart on his nose had grown slightly, but he exuded an expensive cologne, and was wearing a fine suit and a silk top hat as would befit any dandy of the New World.

"Well, I've been lucky with that machine I invented. After that, things just fell my way." Moshko waved over a cab for the journey to Posukeva.

"I knew you'd be a success someday, but this big I didn't know."

"I didn't know either. I guess my soul received a more favorable placement this time around, but I still dream of the sheep and sometimes the rooster too." Moshko laughed. "I got a good brain and a good mother and a good uncle, may he rest in peace. Uncle Heschel thought I could accomplish anything, if I put my mind to it."

"He was so proud of you, and he loved you so much."

"I was sorry to leave him, I know how much he wanted me to take over the business, but in the end, he encouraged me to go. He knew that the shtetl was dying."

"He wrote the doctor several times to tell him how Shaina missed out."

"I know," said Moshko.

The drosky stopped at their little house, and Moshko gave the man a two-ruble tip, a week's worth of wages in his old job. The place hadn't changed much in the eight years that he'd been gone, except for the for-sale sign on the front porch.

"Remember Hanna Averbuch?" asked Luba.

"Yes, I do, she was in love with the potato maven."

"The wedding fell through when the farmer got cold feet. She tells me she's still available."

"Available?"

"Yes, she's ready for marriage to you, preferably before you leave, and she has a for sale sign on her house too."

"But I'm too short, there's the problem with the wart on my nose, and I'm too fat."

"That doesn't seem to matter anymore. She'd like you to come by tonight. And you'll never believe this?"

"Believe what?"

"Remember Mindel Zipursky?"

"The rabbi's daughter?"

"Well somehow, she's heard about the machine that you invented, and last month, she made a trip from Nemirov with her father, just to see me."

"So?"

"They both wanted to tell me that Mindel liked you very much. Her father says it's best if she emigrates to America, and they'll go with her. She won't even care if you eat bacon with your breakfast."

"I keep kosher Mama, so she wouldn't need to worry." Moshko looked around the cottage and peeked into his old bedroom. The bed and chest of drawers were gone.

"I'm sorry, I've sold most of the furniture and the kitchen utensils. I don't even have food for dinner."

"That's okay Mama, we have some guests coming. We'll eat at the inn."

"Guests?"

"A woman and her father. She was singing in a band that came to Cleveland one day, and I met her behind the stage after the show. One thing led to another, and they're going to meet me here."

"A band? Is that the right girl for you, now that they're standing in line?"

Just then there was a knock on the door. It was Shaina, and Hymie was with her. She rushed over to Moshko and gave him a kiss on the lips then a little peck on his nose right where the wart resided, and they laughed and they laughed. Hymie laughed too, and so did Luba.

Heel of Souls

Paul Cohen felt a sensation behind his sternum, like a glowing ember. He'd just ingested eight pork medallions in spicy mustard sauce, a mound of pomme frites, fresh asparagus splashed with balsamic vinegar, and an entire basket of buttery soft rolls. After the dinner plates had been cleared, he and Callie had talked and talked over the crème brulee and a second bottle of Bordeaux as they viewed the faux Eiffel tower from their window table. Her perfect lips loosened as the two of them chatted about her future with Midtown Podiatrists Inc.

Paul excused himself and texted Murray from the men's room. *I can't do it tonite, she's sloshed.* There was no reply. Murray Gutfriend, Paul's partner, had also planned to attend the Foot and Ankle Association's convention in Las Vegas, until he realized that the first day of the conference overlapped with the second night of Passover. Paul surmised that Murray would look at the text after the Seder ended, the participants having imbibed the traditional four glasses of wine, except of course, the one reserved for Elijah. Paul smiled wryly. He was Jewish too, at least he was born Jewish. His mother was a nonbeliever and his father, a two-day attender at the synagogue: only on the High Holidays. Paul had been bar mitzvahed, but after he married Mary Catherine Kitty O'Donnell, he checked the box of the religious unaffiliated. He didn't believe in prophets or angels.

Callie and Paul had spent the entire day at the meeting. They'd listened intently as the latest techniques in removing corns and bunions were discussed by a blue-ribbon panel of eminent podiatrists, or at least Callie did. Paul found himself dozing off. Expositions on toe excisions did that to him. The next session was entitled, "Diagnosing tarsal fractures using high resolution MRI technology." Paul had put his hand on Callie's inner thigh as images of trapezoid foot bones paraded across the screen. She didn't remove it, in fact, she looked over at him once or twice as the reflected silver light from the MRI images illuminated those glossy lips.

"Why don't we go up to my room for a nightcap." Paul poured the last of the wine into Callie's glass.

"You'd rather be with me than play blackjack?" Callie frowned playfully as Paul stared at her exquisite Nordic arms exposed by her sleeveless dress.

"What do you think?" He reached across the table and grasped her hand. The full softness of her skin was that of a young woman. Paul felt desire rising in him. "Anyway, the action doesn't start until midnight."

"Could I bring my expansion plans for the office? If we take over the space next door, we'll be able to service our patients more efficiently."

"Sure Callie, we could." There was an edge in his voice. An ulterior motive for her flirting irritated him, but then why would a beautiful accomplished young woman go to bed with an overweight old fart like himself?

"And I have some other ideas, too."

"We'll talk about whatever you'd like."

"I'll get my notes from my room, and put on something more comfortable." Callie laughed and gave him a wink, then she blushed. She got up and gave him a kiss on the cheek, and her lips lingered awhile. "I won't be more than a few minutes," she whispered huskily. Paul paid for the dinner, $350 plus tip, with the Midtown Podiatrists Inc. credit card. After all, they had talked business.

Callie Eriksen had interned with Paul's group two summers ago. He was impressed with her zeal for the profession, and he began to believe that her lithe athletic physique would attract new patients to the practice. She certainly had attracted him. The other partners had been dubious. Their building was located in an older, ethnically mixed part of the city, and many of their patients had fled to the all-white new-construction exurbia. They didn't need another mouth to feed. Nevertheless, Paul was persistent and persuasive. The group finally agreed to open a satellite office in an affluent suburb where Callie could establish a practice of women and younger patients. She eagerly accepted the job offer; her boyfriend, a weight lifter and personal trainer, had just opened his own fitness center a few blocks from where the new office would be located.

She had been with the group but a year, when her soulmate found a different mate, a wealthy divorcee with freshly minted boobs and buttocks. Paul was there to pick up the pieces. His affair with the office scheduler had ended precipitously when she ran off to Colorado with the rough-hewn plumber who'd maintained the whirlpool tank in the office. Paul dangled the possibility of a fast-track partnership with a generous $200,000 compensation, if only Callie would do him some favors once in a while.

Paul's personal expenses had grown exponentially in the past year. He carried over $80,000 on his credit cards, paying the annual interest of 18%. Their son, Stevie, was in law school at the University of Chicago with an annual tuition of 65,000 smackers, and Molly planned to attend Vassar in the fall. Kitty had redecorated the living room with hardwood floors and Persian rugs, showering the walls with expensive art work for the chic parties that she loved to host. In September, they'd vacationed at the finest hotels in Rome, Florence and Milan along with a week on Lake Como. Last week, she announced that the backyard deck needed to be re-built, the swimming pool had developed a crack, and the two large pine trees in the backyard would have to be cut down before the they fell on the house, and no, it couldn't wait until next year. The more he cheated, the more she seemed to spend. He frequented his favorite casinos, trying to gamble his way out of debt, but his previous skill seemed to vanish, digging him deeper in the hole. That's when he decided to steal from the practice.

A month before the Foot and Ankle convention, the four partners held the annual pre-tax meeting with their accountant. Expenses had mushroomed owing to Paul's diversion of practice funds to pay his personal debts, debts that he recorded as expenditures for the new office. As the managing partner, Paul, and only Paul, signed the checks, so that the living room sofa and chairs were listed under *structural improvements*, the airfare to Italy was placed under *salaries*, and the LeRoy Neiman original water-color was expensed as *equipment purchases*. When the others realized that there was no money for the yearly bonuses, there were three stinking-mad foot doctors at Midtown Podiatrists Inc. Despite Paul's vehement objections, they sought to close the new office and terminate Callie's contract. It was only after they submitted their resignations that Paul acceded to their demands. He would break the bad news to her at the seminar, but he had no intention of spoiling their affair this evening.

Callie arrived at Paul's room wearing a braless tank top and a very short pair of short shorts. She was carrying a loose-leaf note book and a makeup bag. "You don't mind if I spend the night?" She smiled, revealing the perfect white teeth of a Viking.

"That'd be just great, more than great." Just then, another burning flash scalded his chest. God dammit, why was he such a glutton.

"I hope you brought some Viagra for the trip," she giggled, a little embarrassed.

"Just because I'm 56 years old doesn't mean I need something like that." He forced a chuckle and gave her a clumsy bear hug, nuzzling his face towards her for a kiss. She pushed him away.

"First, I want to present my ideas." She reclined her shapely thighs on the bed and opened her notebook.

"How many pages?" he asked.

"This will take about thirty minutes." His heart was pounding with excitement, and he was strangely short of breath.

"Sure, honey, go ahead. I'll take an antacid. The pork's given me indigestion." Paul went into the bathroom and took a Zantac along with a Viagra. He came back and sat on a chair near the bed.

"Well, first off, let's talk about the new space," said Callie. "I've checked with the landlord and they're charging twenty dollars a square foot. With the additional one thousand square feet, that comes to 20k a year, add in painting and carpeting, and we're looking at another fifteen or twenty thousand, plus we'll need to add a second receptionist and a part-time physical therapist."

"You've got this all planned out, don't you?" Paul forced some enthusiasm. He needed to perform this ritual before his admittance to Callie's magnificent temple.

"We'll have to upgrade our website. My idea is to play mini podcasts of the partners, highlighting their areas of expertise. They'll begin talking after clicking on their photos. You could talk on hammer toes, Murray on heel blisters, Philip on callouses, and Ashfaq could have a dialogue on plantar fasciitis."

He suddenly felt tired as the five glasses of wine worked on his brain. He'd gambled until 2 a.m. the night before. "Sounds fantastic, just great."

"The Kingston group is excellent. They'll do the website for $3,000. Jack Shapiro works at Microsoft, and he'll freelance the work for a lot less. And of course, Billie down the hall is very talented...Paul, are you listening?"

"I'm sorry, please go on."

"Now, about the new surgery suite. You know the Bovie we're using for electrocautery is outmoded. It keeps shorting out and we've called the rep five or six times but without an upgrade..."

Paul clutched his chest. His heart was palpitating and his lips were gray. "Callie, couldn't this wait for a bit, the indigestion..."

"I'm almost done. Here, try a few of my Tums. I always bring three basic meds, Advil, Nyquil, and Tums, and Band Aids, I never forget those. Then there's the spa that we'd build, specially designed for the working woman and her feet... Paul, Paul!"

⌒

A haze of smoke wafted through the room. Paul was disoriented. He could have sworn that the outside door was located on the opposite wall. Fresh, pale-pink sheets were silky soft to his naked body. He reached over to touch Callie but she was gone. He put on his pajamas and slippers, neatly piled at the end of the bed. He shuffled over to the door and opened it a crack. A torrent of fire rushed at him. He slammed it shut. Paul hunted for the fire alarm, but couldn't find it in the darkness. In panic, he made a run for his life. The flames had died, and the corridor was filled with cinders and ashes. There were two deep grooves in the debris as if a vehicle had passed through.

Paul, in his flip-flops, stumbled awkwardly in the tracks until his way was impeded by a wall of large limestone blocks piled on one another. There was a square piece of glass wedged in a crack between the largest stones. He pulled a crumpled Kleenex from his pajama bottoms and wiped the soot from its surface. It was a portrait of a wizened man with a long beard and an outsized hooked nose that could have hung an overcoat. He was holding a book in one hand, and there was another on a desk in front of him.

"Hello, Saul." The voice startled him, but there was no motion of his lips.

"Where am I?"

"You're in the hereafter, Saul."

"I must be dreaming."

"This is a holding area for the deceased. You'll stay here until I'm receiving further orders."

"It can't be."

"In regards to earth, you're dead. You're just a soul that once treated soles, Saul." There was a cackling laugh.

"The name is Paul."

"Saul, Paul, Raul, it's all the same."

"Who the hell are you?"

"Gallizur, a low-level angel, a *nebbish*. I'm a nebbish angel."

"You're Jewish?"

"What, a saint you expected?"

"But I don't practice Judaism, I don't go to synagogue or follow any customs or celebrate any holidays…"

"It doesn't matter, your soul is Jewish going back as far as anyone can calculate. There's no soul that's an atheist."

"How come your lips don't move and you don't breathe?"

"That's because there's no dimension of time. We're in infinity. When something moves over time, it travels from point A to point B. One second my lips are making a sound of an *o*, the next second a *p*, then an *e*. When there's no ticking of a tock, movement you won't detect, like a still photograph."

"But your voice?"

"What voice? It's a communication device that's not present on earth. *Farshtaist?* It's a Yiddish word meaning *understand*. A freight train I could sound like, or a lion, or the ocean, but to you, I'm an old Jewish man speaking broken English. When we communicate in the afterworld, it's just farshtaist."

"Where do I go from here?" asked Paul.

"Gehenna."

"Gehenna?"

"That's another thing, some people call me the angel of bad news."

"So, I'll be going to …"

"You think somewhere else? You want *heaven*?" The old man chortled.

"Sure, there's been some bumps along the way, some things I'm not proud of, but I've spent my life devoted to helping those afflicted with bad feet. Do you have any idea what's it's like to have a painful corn on your fifth toe? No, you wouldn't, living inside a picture frame. I've got testimonials from people and if I could…"

"Are you remembering Rosh Hashanah last year?"

"Are you *remembering?*" Paul was skeptical.

"You were in Las Vegas again, gambling and fornicating. For the evening you hired a call girl, then to poor Kitty you lied. If you'd been a Menahem Greenbaum who ate a Christian chicken at Chick-fil-A, or a Joseph Kaplan on the Sabbath driving his Tesla, or a Sylvia Finkel on the seventh day of Passover sneaking a stale bagel, a pass you might have got. You could have been written in The Book of Life. But after the performance you gave, no way. To top it off, on Yom Kippur you had unkosher thoughts concerning your neighbor."

"Tricia and I are good friends, her husband's constantly travelling for business. I went over there to attend to her in-grown toe nail."

"That's commandment Number Ten, you might have forgotten. That you shall not covet your neighbor's wife, ox, or ass. You're a sinner Paul, a dime a dozen sinner that passes through here like a clockwork."

"What happens now?" Paul's voice quavered.

"To the angels in Gehenna, I'll turn you over. They'll rough you up pretty good. You'll scream in anguish. It'll feel like a screw turning in your brain, a poker sticking your eye, a red-hot torch scorching your skin; only a screw, a poker, a torch there isn't, and a brain, an eye, and a skin you don't have. Your soul will wander the world and angels will toss it back and forth like a plastic frisbee. And who knows how long it will take to sanitize it, like it's been to a dry cleaner. Then it will be placed in cold storage till we need it again."

"But if I could just go back and straighten things out."

"What are you talking *straighten things out*? You're in the Book of Death, Saul, the one on the table. You're sealed, like a beetle crawling on a driveway when asphalt is poured. You think someone should give you a second chance?"

There was a flickering of the image. Horizontal lines buzzed back and forth in the glass, like a television set from the nineteen sixties gone on the blink. "Wait, I'm getting a farshtaist from the higher-ups, it's from Elijah."

"I thought I saw your lips move. This thing is all a dream, a hoax."

"It's about your soul, something strange."

"My rotten soul, eh. Maybe I haven't been so bad after all." Paul laughed derisively.

"Goodbye Saul."

‿〜

Paul was in another chamber still wearing his pajamas. The floor was purple velvet. Pictures of pink flamingos adorned chartreuse walls. A gigantic creature wrapped in a stunning azure garment stood under a spotlight. It wore a carrot-colored wig, thick orange lipstick, and white powdered cheeks. Outrageous sapphire earrings dangled from outsized ears.

"Who are you?" Paul inquired.

"I'm Elijah, couldn't you have guessed? Sorry, the chariot took a wrong turn and crashed into the Wall." Elijah put their hand on their waist, did a little bump with their hips and grinned. "I'm not much of a driver, I get distracted and all. I really don't need a chariot to get around, a bald eagle or a big black handsome raven would suffice. Hey, nice pajamas Paul, I like the mauve elephants. Then, guess what? I had to fetch some chicken soup for The Messiah, nice and salty, with carrots, celery and unhatched chicken eggs, floated some matzo balls too, for Passover. I got myself a rum and coke, I don't even drink wine as you might have guessed." Elijah roared and Paul shrank back.

"You know The Messiah? He's been chained to his throne for all these centuries. He suffers in pain, so so much. He sobs all of the time for the world, Paul, for the world. He rambles on about Jews like you: lying, stealing, womanizing. And greedy, my goodness! Is there no charity for the poor, the hungry, the oppressed, and the diseased? Have we forgotten the agony of the Holocaust? It will be difficult repairing this Covid-invested, ice-melted, polluted world. And who will listen? People are on their cell phones, texting and tweeting and playing video games and thinking they're rich, but they're not Paul, they're not. He wants so badly to return to earth and that's where you come in Paul, or at least your soul does. Actually, just a spark, a small spark. There are 600,000 Jewish souls descended from Adam, the same number as the letters in the Torah. When the population of Jews exceeded that number, only sparks of souls were given out by God, and I need a certain glimmer from your wretched soul Paul, your wretched soul. Without that one little spark, the Messiah can't be freed. It's all going to be so difficult.

Only God knows how to get this done. But he's so far away and so hard to find, like a diamond in a universe where there's an infinite number of universes. He must have been hiding your speck of a spot of a spark until just the right time."

"My spark?"

"It turns out you have an exceedingly special spark from a pious relative, Rabbi Shaul Cohen who lived centuries ago. I'll combine it with the souls of the greatest Jewish sages that ever lived. Then I'll be able to release the Messiah from his shackles."

"I'll die and you'll have a bit of my soul so that the Messiah can make his appearance?"

"Something like that."

"And what will happen to the rest of me?"

"Like Gallizur told you, the rest of your soul will be stowed away in something like a warehouse. When I've rounded up all the spirits that ever lived, the Messiah will reveal himself. I'll blow the shofar to signal the End of Days, and everyone will be living in the Garden of Eden again, except for the snake, he's been disqualified. It'll take me at least seven years, maybe seven hundred, to find all the souls, even those that have transmigrated into fish, lions, monkeys and rocks."

"Rocks?"

"Rocks, stones, sticks, even an aluminum can or two. When I lived on earth twenty-five hundred years ago, we owned a dog. This creature sat at my father's death bed, didn't eat or drink for five days after Dad passed away. His soul was taken back to heaven and eventually, an itty-bitty bit was taken up by David ben Gurion, the first Prime Minister of Israel."

"I'll need your body too, after we get your heart working again. I can't come down to fix things looking like this, can I?" Elijah did a backflip followed by a cartwheel. Paul heard a drum roll.

"How come you can move and Gallizur?"

"Time is created by the truth of the righteous, Saulie-boy."

"But why can't you just take my spark and return me to earth? I'm sure I can manage without it. I can repent. I'll talk to the partners tomorrow, I'll work for nothing until I pay them every penny that I stole. I'll tell Callie how I admire her as a woman and a doctor, and that she'd do well to be free of me and my filthy operation. Then I'll go home and beg Kitty for forgiveness, come clean about my philandering, and profess how much I love her. I'll work in a free clinic. I'll minister to the feet of the poor, the hungry, the downtrodden, and the weary. I'll attend synagogue. I'll wear a yarmulke and a tallit and pray every day. I'll study the Talmud. I won't eat another pork steak or even a strip of bacon and no mixing the milk with the meat. Just give me a little more time. I'll be redeemed before you ever set foot on earth."

"But Saulie, how can you reform without that spark when you were a sinner *with* it?"

"You'll see what I can do. Just try me, just give me a second chance. You owe me something for filching my flicker."

⤿

Paul's eyes opened as the faint rays of dawn lighted his hotel room. He heard Callie's breathing next to him. He lay back on the pillow and looked up at the ceiling. He recalled the fire and the chariot tracks, the angel in the glass window, and the creature with the orange wig that had occupied his dreams. Thank God, he hadn't really died. He chuckled that he'd *thanked God*, but maybe he should come clean with Murray and the others. He might call Kitty and the kids today. And when he got back, he could talk to the rabbi who lived on their street, but he'd forgotten his name. He looked over at the ravishing semi-nude Callie, and his eyes widened.

He heard the toilet flush. Alarmed, he jumped up and ran to the bathroom. In the dimness, he thought he saw someone who looked like himself, sitting on the toilet and jangling the handle, before flushing it again and again. Paul flipped the switch on the wall, and bright light from the LED fixtures flooded the room. He noticed an empty roll of tissue lying on the floor, but there was no one sitting on the toilet and the flushing had stopped. He looked in the vanity mirror; there was nobody there, not even himself. He dived back into bed, pulled the pale pink sheets over his head, and tried to go back to sleep before sinking into the abyss.

The Dybbuk of Brooklyn

Several years ago, a dybbuk came to live with me, or to be more specific, inside of me. For the uninitiated, a dybbuk is a phantasmagoric spirit first described by Jewish mystics in the sixteenth century. I'd always assumed this was a *bubbe-meise* (grandma's tale), until I had the misfortune of cohabitating with one. Of course, it's possible that I had a bout of insanity, but I've been off my anti-psychotic medications for almost a decade, and once Meshulam stopped wrestling with my soul, he never bothered me again.

It all started with a dream that took place in a dusty tavern in Olgopol, a shtetl near the Black Sea. My family's been in the liquor business in Brooklyn for three generations, and before that in the old country, so dreaming about saloons wasn't all that unusual. A bartender was serving shots of vodka to two men dressed in long black coats and big black hats, with sidelocks curling around their earlobes, and scraggly beards hanging like vines past their chins.

"This stuff has a kick, a zetz," said Hasid One as he took a swig. "Where'd you get that?"

"None of your business," said Meshulam Goldfeld, the bartender.

"Bootleg?" said Hasid Two.

"Not I," said Meshulam.

"Okay, then it was your brother, Gershon. The whole town knows it." This was uncomfortable. I'd just starting dreaming, and already my relatives were bootlegging. Sure, my Dad and uncle did some shenanigans years ago, hiding some income from the tax man, writing off some vacations as business trips, even importing some knockoff wines as the real McCoy, but never bootlegging.

"We'd like to try some of that German wine that our friend, Chechelnik, drank here last week. Smuggled that in I guess?" Hasid Two laughed. Smuggling AND bootlegging, this was serious.

"What do you want me to do?" Meshulam retorted. "Legally, I'm supposed to buy all my wine and vodka from Meyer Kagan who's been granted the liquor monopoly by the Russian authorities. He's marking up his wholesale vodka to the moon. How can I compete with taverns in Bratslav or Tulchin?"

Hasid One took a taste of the spatlese and smiled. "Smooth as silk," he said.

"It's not kosher," said Meshulam, "but I guess you fellows drinking in a tavern isn't kosher." They laughed.

Just then, the door flew open and three Russian policemen burst in bearing muskets. "Goldfeld, we've got an order for your arrest."

"And why may I ask?"

"For the unapproved production and importation of alcohol." They examined the vodka and wine bottles on the bar. Irrationally, Meshulam ran for the door. Then the gun went off.

෴

I bolted up in bed. I was back in my one-bedroom apartment in Brooklyn, January 31, 1965. It was a silly nightmare, like sitting for my biology final and realizing that I'd studied for the chemistry exam, or running naked in the streets, trying to remember where I lived. I settled under the blankets and slept till the polluted light of day streaked into my bedroom, then I arose to pee and brush my teeth.

Suddenly, I heard a voice speaking in a thick European accent. *"Vhere am I? Vhere am I?"* It wasn't the natural thinking voice that goes on in people's brains all day. It felt like a parasite had invaded me, like a bloodsucker on your leg, a tick in your ear, or an angry dachshund latched on to your ankle. *"Hello! Anybody home? This is Meshulam, Meshulam Goldfeld."*

Sure, I'd been depressed with anger issues and paranoia. I'd snorted cocaine and hallucinated on LSD, but not since I'd flunked out of college. I'll admit to an alcohol and prescription drug problem off and on, and I'd had a few drinks the night before, okay, more than a few with a gal named Pamela that I met at a bar. I'd gone home, drank a glass of milk and found some trazodone in the medicine cabinet to help me sleep. I ignored the warning label as it floated by: DON'T DRINK ALCOHOLIC BEVERAGES WHILE TAKING THIS MEDICINE, but this wasn't the first time I'd mixed drugs and booze.

"Are you the fellow I dreamt about last night?"

"*That's me. I vill be living in your brain, Dybbuk No. 2250-49.*"

"I'm being overrun by an alien?"

"*Only my soul Morrie, the inner part, the* **is**. *You'll realize this ven you have the privilege of being dead, and you're not thinking or feeling, just* **ising**."

"How did you end up with me?"

"*After I died from the bullet, my soul was visited by Angel Tzadkiel. He can only be seen in a mirror and a blurry one at that, some people are just shy, but I vouldn't know about angels. Anyvay, he tells me I'm some good, and some not so hot. Think about it. Everyvone has some positives and negatives. You send vone fellow to heaven and one to hell, but most of the time it's a fifty-fifty. You get a Hitler or a Stalin or a serial killer, it's a no brainer, but you get a Meshulam Goldfeld from Olgopol in the province of Podolia, maybe it's not so easy. Hey, it's raining indoors? Vhat the hell is going on!*"

"I'm taking a shower. The water goes into a pipe which empties into a sewer that drains into a water purification plant, then into the East River, and from there to the ocean."

"*Vhat for?*"

"I'm washing to cleanse myself. We do it almost every day in this century."

"*Like a Jewish ritual bath, a mikvah?*"

"Something like that."

"Anyhow this Angel Tzadkiel tells me I'll be a vandering soul, a dybbuk, and that's vat I do."

"What sins did you commit?"

"Stealing, lying, svearing, smuggling, adultery, blasphemy, things like that, but there's lots of positives too. I vas voted the best barkeeper for jokes, three years in a row, and if you vant to get drunk, there vas no better man than me to be pouring you vodka or a viskey."

"Maybe more bad than good."

"Maybe."

"How long will you be attached to me?" Meshulam didn't answer. My head was bursting. I took two aspirins, got dressed and went down the block to the local diner. As I sat down, the dybbuk piped up. *"Vhat? A tavern that has a breakfast?"*

"It's not a tavern, it's a restaurant that serves breakfast and lunch, no alcohol."

Mary greeted me with a menu. She had been a knockout in her twenties, but now there were furrows under her chin, and lines had crept diagonally from the corners of her mouth. She took a five-a.m. subway to get to work six days a week, and she'd raised a son on a lousy waitress salary. We'd had a fling once, but I went back to Elaine, my wife of ten years and my ex-wife of five.

"I'll have two eggs sunny side up and two strips of bacon, please."

"Vhat, pork you eat? You'll do vorse than me vhen you die." I said this aloud even though it was coming from the dybbuk.

"Large or small coffee?" She appeared puzzled at my outburst.

"Large, with two sweeteners."

"Some goat's milk on the side, too."

"Morrie, we don't sell goat's milk." Mary laughed. She thought I was joking. She was still fond of a nobody like me, twelve years older, and a schlump of a liquor salesman, always asking my younger brother, Irving, for an advance on my salary to pay gambling debts and sometimes the alimony. Irv was a saint to keep me on in the business.

"I got a guy inside me that talks when he shouldn't."

"Have you seen your psychiatrist lately?" Her voice was concerned.

*"You von't believe this Morrie. Vhen she laughed, she looked like somvone I know. Just after I died, I vas valking on this very narrow bridge vhen I saw this light, not sunlight, but the light in the first days of the bible ven God said 'let there be light', and then I saw **her.**"* I stared into my empty coffee cup.

"Morrie, are sure you're okay?" She sat down across from me, her eyes so blue with a tinge of sadness, her face soft and sweet, but I'd thought that about Elaine too, once upon a time, like a fucking fairy tale gone bad. And I'd gone back to Elaine like a fool, a schlump supreme.

Now, I was afraid to speak, afraid of what would come out, with meshuga Meshulam lurking inside me. I wolfed down my food and paid the bill at the cash register. I waved to Mary on the way out. Meshulam was now shouting inside. *Let me talk! I vant to talk vid her!* I made an odd squeaking noise, a sibilant whistle, as I tried to repress the bastard.

"It vas Bessie, Baruch the butcher's vife from Babanochka. I saw her at the end of the bridge."

"Look, I don't have time for your shit. Keep quiet or I'll put a gun to my head and pull the trigger, and we'll both be dead. How about that? If I blow out my brains, then where are you going?" The voice went quiet.

I entered a warehouse on Henry Street, one of those red brick structures that are a dime a dozen in the Red Hook district. There was a sign, *Goldfine Wine & Spirits* on the door. I went into my brother's office. Irv was on the phone. He was shorter than me with stubble on his face and a rumpled suit. "I'll send Morrie over right away," then he hung up.

"We've got a problem over at Gibson's. They claim we shorted them on the whiskey order, and by the way, you're two hours late."

"I didn't sleep well, nightmares."

"God damnit Morrie, I can't keep you on the payroll if you don't put in a decent day's work."

"You let this punk talk to you with such a voice?"

"What did you say?"

"I'll get right over and talk to Al."

"I guess you've had one or two over there, huh?" Irv chuckled.

"Guess so."

"Maybe if you cut out the off-hours in the bars and put more time in the in-hours, things would go a lot smoother. We've lost two big accounts this month already. Are you taking your medicine Morrie?"

"What makes you think I'm not?"

"You're making hissing noises."

"Something's going on in my head, that I'm trying to suppress."

"Quaaludes? Vallies?"

"Not that."

"When did you last see Dr. Baumgartner?"

"A month ago, everything was fine. You don't understand. This is different. Say hello Meshulam."

"Hello Irv, I'm a landsman from the shtetl. If your grandfather vas alive, he'd tell you all about his great uncle from Olgopol. I'm just passing through, I'm hoping to get from A to B, it's a long story."

"Geez Morrie, are you sure you can work today? I could call a cab to take you home. I can send Bobby."

"Believe me, as long as I make those noises, he'll keep quiet."

Fifteen minutes later, we'd entered Gibson's Bar in Park Slope. "You guys trying to short-change me or what?" Al got right to the point.

"Let me see the invoices." I said.

"You don't believe me?"

"That's not it, I just have to write up a report and we'll get the whiskey to you this afternoon."

"In the old country, ve call in Shmelik Ratmansky and his boys, and ve break legs. No vone complains after that."

"What the hell are you talking about Morrie?" Al was getting hotter.

"Hey, just kidding, I'll get right to it."

⟿

That evening, I drank some hot tea and drifted off to sleep. Meshulam was walking on a bridge over a steep abyss, just as he told me. A woman was waiting on the other side. And for a moment, just a moment, she looked like Mary, same face, same melodic voice.

"Meshulam, I've been expecting you."

"Let me explain, Bessie."

"Explain? Explain what? Why you disappeared three days before our wedding? Your mother and father cried, your sisters cried, and I cried for two years until I married Baruch Gitterman, the butcher, and had to clean cow's blood from his boots, and then I cried again."

"But after all these years, vhy now?"

"I know you won't believe it…"

"Vhat's to believe?"

"I still love you. I asked Angel Tzadkiel to make you a dybbuk, a wandering soul. and maybe someday the angel will see to it that you can rest in heaven."

"Do I have a choice?"

"Yes, you do, Meshulam, you can go to Hell for eternity."

⟿

I awoke, my nightshirt soaked with sweat. It was 9 a.m. I'd slept in again.

"I guess ve'll just have to make the best of it. Like Siamese twins joined at the head," offered Meshulam philosophically.

Just then, my cell phone went off. It was Irv. "I know I'm late, I'll be right in," I said.

"Don't bother, you're suspended."

"What?"

"I got calls from three of the clients that you visited yesterday. You're mumbling and talking to yourself. You couldn't go to lunch with Jerry because Meshulam insisted you get a haircut and have your moustache trimmed. You told Jake to find another distributor, one that could supply Ukrainian vodka, and Lou said you made snorting noises, like a bull with a nasal drip."

"I told you, this guy's in my brain. Can I help it if he's a loud, complaining Jew?"

"You'll be on a leave of absence until I receive clearance from your psychiatrist. I'll pay half your salary until your disability comes through, or Baumgartner gets rid of the voices in your head." Irv hung up. The phone rang again. It was Elaine.

"I just talked to Gloria." Gloria was Irv's wife.

"How's she doing?"

"Gloria's well, it's you that isn't. Irv told her you're hearing voices, and you won't be working for a while."

"I can explain that. I'll get this under control believe me."

"Just like your drinking and the Quaaludes. Just like you wouldn't see that woman Mary again, just like you wouldn't slap me around, just like you wouldn't gamble away your salary. I'll have my lawyer call your lawyer if you dare stop the alimony payments—" I hung up. There's only so much you can hear from a woman, particularly when most of it's true.

‿ᔑ

The next day, I was sitting on Baumgartner's couch.

"Elaine called me. She said it was an emergency. What's going on, Morrie?"

"Someone's taken up residence in my head."

"You're hearing voices?"

"Of course, I hear his voice when he speaks to me, but we've come to an accommodation. He's only going to talk if there's no one around, otherwise he needs my permission. He's my great-great uncle from Olgopol. Say hello to the doctor, Meshulam."

"Hello doctor. I understand you're a psychiatrist. Ve didn't have any of those in the shtetl, maybe some bigshot doctors in Odessa, but not in Olgopol. The great Freud didn't develop his theory of the unconscious until 1900, just before I died. Morrie is a vise and a clean man, that I can tell you, and he's fit as a fiddle. I think ve can vork things out, but I have to admit that this voman he's was married to is one hell of a bitch, she never gave the man a chance to show his good side for even vone minute. He's paid alimony five years, hardly missed a payment and okay, he got a little rough from time to time and maybe it vas from too much pills or viskey, but I can tell you—"

"Morrie, I think I've heard enough."

Baumgartner looked at his watch. Damn, if your job is so boring that you look at your watch forty times a day, you should try dermatology or maybe take a look in someone's colon, that would keep you awake.

"You're suffering from depression with psychotic symptoms. Hearing voices is a symptom of psychosis. I can tell you that the odds of a little man with a European accent living in your brain, even a Jewish man, is infinitesimally small. I'm going to start you on chlorpromazine, the side effects include dizziness, dry mouth, constipation, weight gain, fatigue—"

⌒

A few days later, I was sitting at the diner eating my usual. Meshulam was complaining about the lack of herring or even a sardine on the menu. *Vhere is that thick rye bread that my mother vonce baked and a raspberry jam? You call this a coffee, it tastes like mud, you should order some tea vid milk.*" Sometimes the dybbuk needed to vent. I put my head on my folded arms and closed my eyes.

"Morrie?" It was Mary. I lifted my head. She had a worried look, like she cared.

"I saw the psychiatrist. His says that the dybbuk residing in my head is a sign of psychosis, but I'm not sure I believe that."

"Psychosis, oh, my!" Her blue peepers alternated between sympathetic and melancholy.

"He started me on a new medication. I felt so groggy this morning."

"*Yeh, it took forever for him to get out of bed, and he hasn't pooped for three days,*" pitched in Meshulam.

"But guess what? I've been doing some searching in the Jewish newspapers, and I found an advertisement from a rabbi who can perform an exorcism."

"*Mary, vould you take me in?*"

"Sure, I'd take you Meshulam, you're my kind of guy. You can't make a living and you're always bitching." They laughed.

"His name is Rabbi Rabinowitz. Should I check him out?"

"Why not Morrie? What harm could it do?"

"It could do plenty harm. See that trash can over there? I could be living in there by next veek."

⤿

I had a real doozy of a dream that night. Meshulam, now just a skeleton, was back on the bridge over the gorge. The rickety structure swayed as a sharp wind came up and rain pelted down. The worn wooden boards became slippery, and all at once, he was in free fall. The primordial light faded as his head spun in the blackness. He landed on a cement floor, his bare bones clattering painfully on the hard surface.

I awoke momentarily, tossing and turning and kicking off blankets. I looked at the clock—it was 3:45 a.m. I rolled on my right side and went back to sleep.

Meshulam looked up and saw a face floating towards him. It had the look of a dried prune. It was Esther, his wife of forty-seven years. But the flat nose, the high cheek bones, and the wart on the chin, could have been, oh God-forbid, Elaine.

"I've been expecting you Meshulam."

"Everyvone's been expecting me. I didn't realize there was so much anticipation of expecting."

"I've been calculating your sins in regard to me, our children, and the human race, and you might be surprised to find out that it's come to an infinite number."

"Do you have an adding machine down here to help vid the calculations?" Meshulam's mandible rattled sardonically.

"The physical abuse, the shouting and screaming, the drinking, the gambling, the philandering …"

"I plead guilty, guilty to everything. I repent. I'd give you a pound of flesh, but look at me."

"You deserve to be in the deepest pit of Hell for eternity, a dybbuk isn't punishment enough for the likes of you!"

My cell phone rang. It was mid-morning. I blinked a few times and tried to focus. It was Elaine. "Is the medicine helping, Morrie?"

"I've only been on it a few days, Esther."

"Esther?" queried Elaine.

"She's my ex-wife," interrupted Meshulam. *"A voman whom I sadly misinterpreted during forty plus years of a loveless marriage."*

I suddenly felt a severe cramp in my lower gut. At least the laxative was working.

⌒

I took the subway up to the Bronx, walked three blocks, climbed five flights of stairs, and knocked ten times. A wizened man, wearing a skull cap over curly grey hair, opened the door. There was a musty smell in the place, like a person hadn't opened a window for a number of years.

"I'm Rabbi Rabinowitz, Reuven Regemelech Rabinowitz, my parents had a penchant for alliteration." There was a Jewish nod of the head, and a smile formed around his mouth. "So Morrie, you're here for an exorcism?"

"Yes. Meshulam is living in me, and he's driving me crazy."

"Like I told you over the phone, this will cost you three thousand dollars. Even a rabbi has to eat, and occasionally take in a Broadway play."

I handed over a roll of bills. "My brother Irv gave me an advance on my salary. I won't be eating for the next ten years." The rabbi didn't laugh. He stuffed the bills in an old valise.

"Can I hear from him?"

"Who?"

"The dybbuk, the third party."

"I'm here under a very extreme protest. Vat do you vant?"

"I'll ask you politely, Meshulam. Please leave this man." His voice lost its affability and became firm, almost as if Moses was addressing his people. "You will reside here temporarily until I can put you up for adoption." He pointed to a tank where some guppies and a few swordtails were darting back and forth.

"You can ask all you vant, but I'm not budging. I like this man and ve're blood relatives, that is, if I had any blood."

"It's easier on everybody if you go quietly. I'll say a few prayers and boom, you'll be out. If you put up a fuss, well, I have some other prayers that will put you into eternal purgatory, as has been suggested by your former girlfriend and your former wife. I guess you realize they weren't the best of references."

"*My God, you know about that?*"

"And as for you Morrie. You're a nonbeliever. It's people like you that are prime targets for dybbuks. These spirits never reside in the religious. I bet you don't believe that Moses parted the Red Sea, do you?"

"No, that's a fairy tale, for sure," I said.

"How about Elijah going up to heaven in a chariot?"

"No chance of that, it's against the laws of physics."

"Well then, how did a dybbuk, a relative from a hundred years ago, get in your brain?"

I had to think about that. "You're telling me that if I believe every word of the bible, then Meshulam will be gone? I'm sorry, but I'm somewhat skeptical."

"Believe me, I'm a professional," said the rabbi confidently.

And so, it happened. The rabbi opened an ancient book that smelled like crumbled gorgonzola. He put on a special white robe and started to chant, and for three thousand dollars he chanted his heart out. I heard splashing, and I looked over at the fish tank. The fish were in a frenzy, like when food is being fed. Then there was silence.

"Is that it?"

"That's it," said the rabbi with a smile.

"Meshulam, Meshulam are you still there?" There was silence.

‿

The next morning, after a splendid, blissful sleep, I was a new man. I rushed over to the diner to talk to Mary. I wanted to tell her about the exorcism, and my determination to have faith in God, and that maybe, just maybe she'd be my girlfriend again.

Mary wasn't there. There was a large Puerto Rican woman in her place named Valentina.

"Where's Mary?"

"She gone, senor."

"Gone?"

"She move away."

"Staten Island or New Jersey?"

"Alaska, she moved to Alaska with her boyfriend. She ain't never coming back."

⌐

It's been almost fifteen years since the dybbuk lived with me. Oh sure, I kept my appointments with Dr. Baumgartner and watched him study his new Rolex watch, which he could afford after all my visits. Those dreams about Esther and Bessie frightened me, and now that I believe in Hell, I really don't want to go there. I got back to work and kept my head down. Irv promoted me to vice-president, and I retired with a watch almost as nice as Baumgartner's.

I joined the rabbi's congregation and attend synagogue regularly. He always told me that Meshulam was his all-time best exorcism, and that he, Rabbi Rabinowitz, should be in the Exorcism Hall of Fame, a big joker that Rabinowitz, for his own jokes. When he moved to a retirement home, the rabbi gave me the fish tank. He told me that Meshulam went through five fish before he finally left. Rabinowitz postulated that he lived in a spruce tree for a while, and then served one year in Hell to complete his punishment. I hope to God that Meshulam has finally made it to heaven.

And I never stopped dreaming about Mary. One sad day, Valentina told me that she had died in a boating accident during the salmon run. Even though she wasn't Jewish, the rabbi convinced Angel Tzadkiel to make her into an *ibur*, a gentle spirit. And guess what? Last year she came to live inside of me.

Lilith's Daughter

Chip Brick blinked and grimaced. A rivulet of angry sweat had escaped from under his baseball cap and entered his left eye; cutting grass in the oppressive heat of a St. Louis summer was one step from hell. As he maneuvered around the aging firepit, the Toro suddenly whined and spat out a bit of the structure's crumbled masonry. Chip recalled how he and Jessica had worked to build it, and how they'd snuggled in its heat during the cool fall evenings and the mild winter days, but that was before he'd lost his job, before the divorce, and before he needed her child support just to get by. The mower's progress was halted by the root of a rotting dogwood, unleashing a torrent of curse words from Chip. They'd planted that tree as a sapling, on the same day that they'd made their first mortgage payment on the house, with money borrowed from William C. "Chuck" Brick Sr., Chip's father. Oh, he'd had a zest for the future back then, a future that soured like a California lemon, the state where Jessica now resided.

Manny Moskowitz buzzed up from the other side of the chain-link fence, slashing irrepressible dandelions with his weed eater. They waved, and turned off their weapons of grass destruction.

"Hey, Chip, how's it goin'?"

"It's crap, Manny, unadulterated *crap*. Jessica's cutting me off. She's terminating the child support seeing as Olivia's not going to college."

"Legally, she doesn't have to pay you a red cent now that your daughter's eighteen. At least, that's what Jessica's been telling my Ellen."

"That, and a million and one other things have gone to the dogs, including Olivia's dachshund. He's been scooting his butt on the carpet. The vet charged me a hundred smackers this morning, to unplug his anal glands. And tell your Ellen to stop texting the ex-bitch." *Christ, he needed Moskowitz and wife to know all his business?*

"Any chance you'll be going back to work?"

"They're not calling any of us back. There isn't a teamsters' job in the whole state since the self-driving trucks took over. Who needs a goddamned union if there's no human drivers anymore? I don't know what I'll do after Jessica cuts the money."

"Jeez, being married to the president of Zeus Pharmaceuticals, she must be rolling in dough. The guy has got to be pulling down a seven-figure salary."

"She's asked Olivia to move out to San Diego more than once, but you know how kids are nowadays. She's attached to Jimmy Griesedieck, and I guess young love trumps all. She punishes the ex by not living with her, and punishes me… by living with me." Chip grunted. "She got a job at Walgreen's last week, as a checker."

"Who did?"

"Olivia. She used to want to be a professor, doctor, lawyer, teacher, or nurse, and now she's settled for checker. It's all a pile of... poop."

"What is?"

"*Life*, Manny. Life, and the world we live in. Now, if I was a retired pharmacist and married to your Ellen, with two doctors for sons, I might feel differently, but as far as I'm concerned, ex-wives and robots have taken over the world. Where is the respect for the male species?"

"That bad huh?"

"Who'd have thought I'd need money from a woman to pay my bills? A wife who left me for her boss."

"Well, thank God Ellen works for a *woman* at the library." Manny chuckled at this stroke of fortune. "She's thinking of retiring with her bad knee and all."

"So, how's she doing after the surgery?"

"It's slow. The doctors say that some people recover real well from arthroscopic knee surgery, and others it takes time."

Just then a strapping fellow exited the Moscowitz house carrying a pile of garbage bags for the recycling bin. "Who's he?" asked Chip.

"That's Yossel, it's only his second day on the job."

"How much do you pay him?"

"A donation to the synagogue is all Rabbi Slobotnick requests."

"He doesn't charge you anything?" Chip noticed that the fellow's gait was a bit stiff, and his neck lacked flexibility. His face was expressionless. "God damn,

Manny. You've got a robot too! What the hell's the world coming to?"

"He's a different kind of robot."

"Oh?"

"He's a *golem*."

"A golem?"

"He's from Europe, from Prague, the rabbi's home town. A while back, he announced that he was bringing them over. We've got about fifteen working in the congregation."

"Just like that?"

"Slobotnick's a bit of an oddball. We tried for three years to find an American rabbi, but no one applied. We're a small congregation, and the salary's not competitive, so we settled on this guy. The prayers are not what we're used to, and his sermons can put you to sleep, and his..."

"How'd you get one?"

"The golem?"

"Yeah, how'd you get *it*?"

"Ellen is vice-president of the Ladies Auxiliary, and sometimes I think this Slobotnick fellow has the hots for her, but Ellen insists he's a bore. With her knee ailing, the rabbi brought Yossel over a few nights ago. Geez, he talked for over two hours."

"The robot talks?"

"No, Yossel's mute. It's the rabbi that goes on and on. He tells jokes about Jews and pickles and underwear, thinks he's a Jackie Mason. And Ellen laughs. And then he has to eat something. She gave him an egg sandwich and he doused it with ketchup, ketchup! What's a religious guy from Prague know about ketchup? And then he wants a beer and then another. Then he's got to tell me about a company that he read about in *The Wall Street Journal* that's making artificial meat that's kosher. Who ever heard of a rabbi that drinks beer and reads *The Wall Street Journal*? Meanwhile, this Yossel goes to town in the kitchen too, loads up a plate of leftover brisket with parsnips and roasted potatoes. Finally, they polish off the chocolate cake that I bought for Ellen's birthday, the cake I was planning to eat for the rest of the week, 'cause she's on a diet to take weight off her knee."

"The robot eats?"

"It eats and sleeps, but it can't speak."

"So, it's half-human?"

"I guess."

"Can a golem have sex?"

"How would I know? I don't ask it, and it can't answer."

"Does he pee?"

"He does. Ellen is instructing Yossel on how to raise and lower the toilet seat before and after his business, and fix his aim."

"Is he a good worker?"

"You bet. Yossel's got a ton of energy. He vacuumed the house, waxed the floors, and did the wash, all this morning. We don't get him again until next week, but Ellen's knee better get better soon, because the golem's going back to Prague next month for a refurbishing."

The next morning, Chip was glued to the tube, watching his favorite reality TV program. He'd been meeting with his neighbors at the local Starbucks, and they'd raved about the episode where a prostitute stole a wonderfully good man from his wife. Now they were starting a family, and she planned to remain a whore after she delivered their baby. Chip became hooked when the wife, who reminded him of Jessica, turned out to be meaner than the harlot. Too bad he'd had a falling out with the coffee club after he hit on Joanie Larson. What the hell? He was single, she was single. He was just having a little fun.

The old-fashioned wall phone rang. He muted the TV, scraped back the cockeyed kitchen chair that he meant to fix, and picked up.

"Mr. Brick?"

"Yes, Chip Brick, here."

"This is Sally, from Quantum Recruiting. I think we finally found a position for you."

"That's great to hear, Sally."

"Uncle Sam has a job hauling radioactive waste to a dumping facility, and with government red tape and all, they need a human being. As you can imagine, it's a high-paying job, forty dollars an hour."

"Wow, then that's really great news!"

Finally, Chip had something to cheer about. He'd worked all of his adult life in the family trucking firm, Brack and Brick. Five years ago, it had been sold to a conglomerate, who promptly fired all the employees including Chip and his dad, Chuck. After that, Chuck headed to a nursing home with Alzheimer's disease or severe depression, the doctors couldn't be sure. Only after his dad passed away, did Chip discover that Uncle Joe

Brack had won most of Chuck's stake in the firm playing poker over forty years. The business had been valued at five million dollars, but Chip inherited just $200,000, and when you don't work for two years, most of that was gone. His dear mother, Hortense, who'd polished, scrubbed, boiled, baked, washed, and ironed to fill every need of Chuck and Chip, died of heart failure just two weeks after Chuck passed. Died of a broken heart, they said.

That's when Jessica walked out. Just when he needed her the most, or at least he needed her job as a pharmaceutical rep the most. Sure, he was irritable and impotent, liked his socks folded a certain way, and didn't do much around the house except cut the grass. He yelled and hollered, and occasionally got abusive, but God damnit, he was depressed and angry, just like his dad, a chip off the old Brick, as his mother used to say. At least he didn't fire a gun at *his* wife.

"Where's the job?"

"In Nome."

"Nome, like Alaska?"

"Nome, near the Arctic Circle. That's where the new dump site is to be located, where the polar bears lived before they died from heatstroke," she laughed. "They're constructing a road just to transport the material. You'll be allowed home one week a month."

"But I've got a daughter who can't be left for that long without supervision. The, the gas stove could explode, the bathtub might overflow, and the house'll be trashed by a bunch of her misfit friends dropping by at one a.m. She's not capable of taking a dirty dish to the dish-washer, a pair of socks to the washing machine, or a milk bottle to the refrigerator. Her room looks like the Walking Dead shared space there, except they don't have fifteen camisoles, fourteen pairs of tights and thirteen pairs of shoes to leave on the floor. Last week, the dog came out of her bedroom playing with a bra, he was disappointed that it didn't squeak like his other toys. And I fill up her car every week because she hasn't learned to open the gas tank cover. I can't trust her with credit cards or even taking the dog out for a piss. Now she wants an account at Pink, for what? To buy shorts so short they could be two-fingered mittens, or something worse that I don't want to know about. I'm up to my neck in debt with her. She's working a dead-end job at a cash register, and this boyfriend shows up. He doesn't wash his hair and he goes barefoot. I'm not sure that I'm ready to go there."

"Take it. It's the first thing that's come up in four months. Good-bye Mr. Chip."

Olivia walked in as he hung up. "Ready to go where?" She had insisted on purple hair with green streaks. There was a rose tattooed on her right forearm, a sprig of cherries on her left shoulder, while endangered wolverines displayed themselves on each ankle. She would have been beautiful except for the black lipstick and the matching toenails.

"To Alaska, to work."

"What about me?"

"I've been thinking about that. You know your mother wants you to come out to California *so so* much, and I think you should go." Chip put on his saddest face.

"And leave Jimmy? Dad, you some kind of crazy? That's not going to happen. I can move in with Jimmy. His mother's brought it up more than once."

"No, she hasn't, that's a lie and you know it. Why would she block your cell phone if she wanted her son to talk to you so badly?"

"I could live here, and Uncle Norris and Aunt Candice could come by and check on me."

"I haven't talked to either of them since the shouting match with the lawyer about Grandpa's estate, imagine, my own brother threatening me with a law-suit."

"You could hire a housekeeper for me, just like Lakshmi's family did when her parents moved to Kolkata for a year."

"They own forty motels in this country. We're not in their league, Olivia, get real." Olivia didn't hear that. She'd put her ear-phones back in and stomped upstairs to her room. The bedroom door slammed and the walls shook. Just then, he heard the sound of a lawn mower. He saw Yossel cutting Manny's grass, and Chip got an idea.

᠎᠎᠎

᠎᠎᠎᠎

That evening, he invited himself to the Moskowitz abode. He handed Ellen a frozen chocolate mousse cake that he'd bought at Costco. "Sorry it took so long for me to wish you a speedy recovery, but when you're unemployed, everything takes forever." He'd been watching TV twelve hours a day.

"Thanks a lot Chip. I shouldn't be eating this, but a little piece won't hurt me."

"Where's your mechanical man?" asked Chip.

"The robot's tucked in for the night," replied Manny, helping himself to the cake. "He's exhausted from all—"

"He's a golem, not a robot," said Ellen.

"Don't interrupt me when I'm talking Ellen, and we're not supposed to use the word *golem*."

"You told me he was a golem yesterday," said Chip.

"Well, Slobotnick doesn't want the word out. Yossel's a machine that can't talk."

"The first golem was produced by Rabbi Judah Loew of Prague in the sixteenth century," whispered Ellen, as if the world was listening. "The Jews were accused of a blood libel, using Christian blood from a dead girl to bake matzos on Passover. The golem investigated and found out that the corpse had been planted in a Jewish household by an evil priest. The defendants were declared innocent by the emperor."

"You think I could get a hold of one?" asked Chip.

"You'd have to talk to the rabbi," said Ellen. "Most days, Yossel is kept busy by the people in our synagogue, and you not being Jewish and all—"

"It'd be impossible," interrupted Manny.

"I need to find someone to stay with Olivia while I'm gone on my new job."

"Congratulations, Chip," said Ellen.

"Unfortunately, it's in Alaska, and I can't afford a babysitter until my first paycheck comes in."

"Well, Rabbi Slobotnick's coming by tomorrow. He likes to visit his congregants after major surgery and if I talk to him…"

"Arthroscopic knee surgery is major?" queried Manny. "I'll tell him that you're very much interested in Judaism. He might do me a favor seeing that I'm vice-president of the Ladies' Auxiliary."

⌐

The following day, Chip accosted Slobotnick after his visit to the Moscowitz's, and before he got back into his BMW. The rabbi was a short portly man with a knitted skull-cap attached by a bobby pin to a few strands of grey hair. He had squinty eyes and a tremendous nose. He was lugging a bulky briefcase.

"Hi, I'm Chip, Chip Brick."

"Slobotnick, Rabbi Duvid Slobotnick." The rabbi offered a greasy hand that smelled of roasted chicken.

"How's Ellen?"

"Such a fine voman. I'd call her a saint if ve had those in our religion," he chuckled at his drollery, "and not hard to look at." He dropped his voice and looked back at the house. "To put up vid Manny, she's maybe an angel. He's, you know vhat I mean, a schnorrer?"

"He snores?"

Slobotnick guffawed. "No, it's a Yiddish vord, a guy who's a pain in the ass and a freeloader, all at the same time." The rabbi had a tendency to emit some spittle, particularly when he laughed. "Are you the fellow that's interested in Judaism? She mentioned a neighbor."

"I've researched the family name. I believe I had a remote Jewish ancestor, a Stein from Lithuania. When they came to this country, they changed their name from Stein to Brick."

"Yeah, Stein means *stone* or *brick* in Yiddish."

"Rabbi, I thought you might give me some pamphlets, then you could come back and we could discuss things."

"No, ve don't do that kind of thing, Chink. No leaflets or flyers. Ve do have the Talmud, but it comes in 37 volumes." Slobotnick's guffaw was accompanied by spittle and the smell of garlic.

"I could sure use some help, some spiritual guidance. I'm a single parent, and I'll need to be in Alaska in two weeks for a new job, and who's to care for her?" He shrugged his shoulders and smiled wryly. He'd talked to Manny enough times to learn some Jewish mannerisms.

"Vell, ve could set up some sessions, and you could take classes at the Jewish Community Center. Then you could attend Friday night services, start singing some prayers and lighting the sabbath candles, of course no driving your car on Saturdays, and then…"

"I'm intrigued with Yokel, the robot who's been working at the Moskowitz residence."

"Yossel?"

"Yeah, him—you think if I joined the synagogue, sort of provisionally, maybe I could get Yossel over to my house?"

"He's taken, booked solid, like an ounce of cheese for ten crackers, as they say in Prague."

"Any chance of another one being shipped over?"

"I vouldn't know about that Chunk. This one vas made special by my brother, Rabbi Pinchas Slobotnick of

Prague, from a special clay on the banks of the Vltava River. Recently, the authorities caught Pinky digging there, and he vas arrested for trespassing. He's thinking of closing down the business and retiring."

"Business?"

"Business. The business of golems." His fiendish cackle betrayed the possibility that the business might not be as kosher as the poultry he'd just eaten.

"Hey, we've got lots of clay and mud right here along the Mississippi and just about everywhere else."

"That von't vork. There's nothing in the Sefer Yitzirah, the ancient book of creation, that mentions the Mississippi."

"Okay, I won't hold you up any further. I sure hope Ellen gets well fast, she's a real gem."

"Ah, such a voman, like a Ruth or a Rachel. They don't make those kind anymore, and *zaftig*, so much of her too, like my bubbie years ago. But that loafer of a husband hardly leaves the house. He's sits on his tuchus and vatches sports on the television or plays computer chess, and I've never seen such a man to eat like that."

"He likes to bowl."

"So vhat?"

"Why don't I take him to the lanes one day. I'd let you know ahead of time, and then you could have Ellen all to yourself, no questions asked."

"You'd do that for me?"

"Or we could go to a movie, or buy a kosher brisket at Costco. I could make lots of time for you to be alone with Ellen, but there'd be a price."

"A price?"

"Have your brother come to town and make a golem for me."

"But you're not even a Jew."

"Moshe Brikovitch, with a big hat on my head, and a black robe that you'd give me."

"Could ve do the bowling first, and see how it goes?"

"Sure."

Two days later, Chip and Manny bowled three games and then went for a beer. Chip called Slobotnick that evening.

"It vent great," enthused the rabbi.

"What'd you do?"

"Ve talked about the Vomen's Auxiliary and a big fund raiser in the fall, a trivia night vid a silent auction."

"And?"

"And vat?"

"And what else happened? Did you kiss her?"

"In my dreams, but she'd made a vonderful cold borscht, such a refreshing soup I never had for such a hot day! My god, the beets had a taste like the old country, vid the carrots spicy just like bubbie used to make, vid a big lump of sour cream floating on the top. Never before have I eaten such a Jewish soup. And the celery…"

"Manny and I are going to bowl again next week."

"That vill be good."

"So, when will your brother arrive?"

"He vont."

"He vont what?"

"He vont be coming. He's getting a procedure on his gullet. Every vonce in a vhile, he gets a piece of a bagel or a sardine stuck in there, and they have to stretch out his esophagus vid a balloon. At his age, who knows if he'll survive?"

"Well, I guess I just hurt my elbow, and I won't be able to bowl for six months." *No point messing with this joker any longer.*

"Vait a minute. I'll do it vidout my brother. Ve'll make a golem or at least I'll try, but I need you to have von more bowling date vid Moscowitz."

"Will do."

⌐

The following Sunday, Slobotnick was in Chip's backyard with a sack of earth. He was wearing a white robe with a matching white prayer shawl and yarmulke.

"From the Mississippi?" asked Chip as he pointed to the sack.

"Yossel dug it up from the bank." Slobotnick dumped the contents on the small patio surrounding the fire pit, and began to mold the clay into the crude figure of a man.

"It doesn't look like a woman," said Chip.

"A voman? Who said anything about a voman?"

"I don't want a male golem living with my daughter while I'm away. You never know about these robots."

"Ve made a voman at von time, years ago. And you need to believe it, it vas trouble, big trouble. Ve don't make them anymore, just men, Clink."

"It's Chip," said Chip. "You know, I kinda like Ellen too. And when you're back in Prague repairing your golems, I might just come over there myself when Manny is doing the grocery shopping or at a baseball game. On the other hand, I could put in a good word for you. Manny and Ellen haven't been getting along all that well lately. Since Manny retired, he hangs around the house all day and makes a nuisance of himself."

"Okay, okay, ve'll give it a try, but you're on your own after it's done." Droplets of sweat collected on the rabbi's forehead and his hands shook as he formed thick, malapportioned arms and legs, with lopsided breasts.

"That looks pretty awful," observed Chip. A few minutes later, Chip returned with a small naked doll with large blue eyes, thick eyelashes, and a petite figure. There were some dark linear marks on the face where it had been run over by a tricycle. "This is the doll that Olivia slept with for years. I took her clothes off so you could see the shape we need to make. If you shorten the legs, thin the arms, and fix the boobs, it might work."

"Vell, it's your golem, you do vat you vant. I can't guarantee such a job, that's for sure."

Chip took over the sculpting and soon they had a fairly decent female. The rabbi inscribed some Hebrew letters on the figure's forehead, the word *emeth*, which means *truth* in Hebrew. He opened the Sefer Yitzirah, and started to circle clockwise around the figure as he chanted from the text, then he paraphrased from Genesis. "*God breathed into her nostrils the breath of life and voman became a living creature.*"

Suddenly, there was a loud retort, almost like a rifle shot, as flames shot up from the fire pit. Slobotnick retreated, his beefy face turned a doughy white. "Such a noise and a fire has never happened. Pinky told me to stay away from the females." Chip looked at him disdainfully. Like a true American, he'd been lighting fire crackers since he was six.

And as the fire died, a petite young woman emerged. She had honey blond hair, and perfect skin except for the skid marks from the bike. Her eyes were sparkling blue and reflective like the doll, with eyelashes long and curling. She was wearing a short shift that exposed her shapely legs, and her breasts were in perfect proportion.

The suddenly rejuvenated Slobotnick roared with glee. "Ve've got.... a voman! I did it!"

Chip stepped forward, "I'm Chip, Chip Brick. What's your name?" The creature shook her head.

"She's a mute," said Slobotnick, "like Yossel."

"Then she'll be more obedient, to perform any service I might desire." Chip mused aloud.

Slobotnick became serious again, his little eyes narrowed and his giant proboscis twitched. "I don't know Chip. Maybe ve should put her back. Pinky vill kill me if he ever finds out about it."

He removed the Hebrew letters from her forehead, and started walking counterclockwise while chanting the prayer backwards. The little princess didn't budge, a fetching smile fixed on her countenance. Finally, the exasperated rabbi confessed, "I've never put anyvone back, you know. She's all yours." He got in the BMW, screeched the tires, and left.

Olivia appeared from her upstairs bedroom with Jimmy trailing behind. "Who's the little man who drove away in such a hurry?" She stared at the being who came towards her. "And who's this?" The creature smiled. "She looks just like my dolly, just like Barbie, the one that I clutched on the nights when you and Mom argued."

"She'll be helping us out while I'm in Alaska," said Chip matter-of-factly.

"Did you guys pick her up at a bar or something?"

"Something like that."

"Jimmy and I are going to the mall." In Olivia's narcissistic world, that was explanation enough.

⤸

Barbie performed the usual household chores as required, but then Chip added some extra jobs: polishing his shoes, mending his socks, even cutting the grass now that Yossel was performing that task next door. She cooked vegetarian meals, tomatoes and fennel, kale and rice, until Chip insisted on hamburgers and steaks. And like some slaveowners, Chip couldn't keep his mind or his eyes off of her. He dreamed of Barbie on a sunswept beach, in the shower, or in bed with him. He even skulked into her room one night, catching his little toe on the bedpost, and his muffled curse awoke her. As her gaze fixed on him, a force squeezed his chest like a vice, cutting his wind. Stumbling out the door, he thought he heard a giggle from the bedsheets.

Two weeks went by, and Chip was standing outside with Olivia, waiting for the Uber to the airport. "I've put my last five hundred dollars in your debit account for emergencies. With your mother's last check, I paid your health premium, the auto payment, the homeowner's insurance, the mortgage, and the ATT bill with the bundled internet. And don't forget to fill Buster's bowl, one cup of kibble twice a day with a half cup of shredded cheddar cheese. He won't eat anything without the cheese. And Jimmy can't live here while I'm gone. Got all that?"

As Chip rattled on, Olivia's stare was expressionless, in passive-aggressive teenage mode. The Uber drove up, and Chip bent close to kiss her good-bye, but she pulled away and his lips contacted a pocket of humid air. Olivia retreated to the house as the car drove away.

"You didn't even kiss your Dad good-bye," observed Barbie from the doorway.

"You can talk?"

"We're not supposed to with humans around, it's against the rules. I should be more like Yossel, who just eats, works, and then eats some more."

"You know Yossel?"

"Yes, he's from Gynedia too."

"Gynedia?

"That's where I live when I'm not golcming. It's in the Andromeda galaxy. Queen Lilith lives there, Adam's first wife."

"Adam who?"

"Adam, as in Adam and Eve. Before Eve, Adam had a wife named Lilith. She kicked him out because he was basically an ass. He wasn't romantic and he wasn't—" The golem paused, thinking of a word.

"Wasn't what?"

"Do you know all about a man and a woman?"

"Well sure, I'm on the pill. Jimmy and I..."

"Then you'll know what I mean when I say that Adam didn't know how to please a woman. When Adam's second wife, Eve, ate the tainted apple, the women of this world became subordinate to men. Lilith left and settled in Gynedia."

"And Lilith's in charge there?"

"Our constitution states that the sexes are equal, but when the playing field is really equal, women come out on top." Barbie laughed.

"So, what do the men do?"

"There's lots of worker men, blockheads like Yossel. Some men are allowed to take wives, but they have to earn that right. Then there's some like your dad who want to love, but don't know how."

"Dad? The guy that lives here? He wants to love?"

"He's very concerned about your welfare. He's travelling all the way to Alaska to earn money to support you, so give him some credit for that."

"I just never thought of him that way. Making all those rules and curfews and nagging and yelling and lecturing and not listening, *to me*."

∽

The trip from Anchorage to Nome was uneventful. The Nuclear Regulatory Commission had done a thorough job ensuring the safety of Chip's cargo. He had more than enough time to dwell on the unfaithful Jessica, and the disrespectful Olivia. He didn't see the pristine rivers, the white birch, the graceful caribou, or the snow-capped mountains, only the gravel road in front of him.

He called Olivia, once. She was more loquacious than usual, talking about her job, the dog, and how Barbie was teaching her to cook. He wanted to tell her that he missed her, but when you have a daughter like that, and you're a father like that, it's hard. Then out of the blue she said "Anyway, thanks Dad."

"Thanks for what?"

"For looking after me, sort of."

"Well, if you're mother hadn't left, and I hadn't lost my job, and if you'd just listen when I tell you something and pick up your room, things would be so much easier for everyone."

"Bye Dad, I've got to go."

Hey, he was just telling the truth.

Chip returned three weeks later. Olivia was waiting for him at the airport. They briefly hugged, and Chip gave her a perfunctory kiss. This time, his lips contacted dermis. She entered the freeway and sped over to the fast lane. "Hey! You forgot to signal," Chip barked. "Don't assume the other cars know what you're doing. And get those earphones out of your ears."

Buster greeted them at the door. Chip picked him up, and the dachshund enthusiastically licked his face with a nonjudgmental tongue. Barbie was in the kitchen; her long lashes flitted as she looked up from the stove.

"We made a special meal for you, as a homecoming," said Olivia, as they sat down at the dinner table.

Chip washed down the meatballs and spaghetti with a beer. "Hey, this isn't bad for robot cooking," but he avoided the tomatoes and cucumber topped with goat cheese.

"So, what have you been doing while I was away?"

"I'm volunteering at a food bank, and I've applied for junior college in the fall."

"Got any ideas of what courses you'll be taking?"

"Not really, I like English and philosophy, maybe sociology."

"You can't earn a living learning that stuff, but at least it's better than working at Walgreens."

"Next week there's the Gay Pride parade. I'll be going to support my fellow females. Even though I'm not gay, I haven't ruled out bisexual." Olivia tittered.

Chip turned red. "Hanging out with a bunch of queers won't get you anywhere in this world. Someone might take a picture of you and spread it on the internet. As your parent, I'm going to forbid you from going there."

"Dad, you must have forgotten. I'm eighteen and you can't forbid me to do anything."

Barbie intervened. "Olivia's been a real help while you were gone. She's been cleaning her room, and making the salad. She's even learned to load the dishwasher."

"Well, well, if it isn't the *talking* Barbie model. Do you come with the AA batteries or do we plug you in?"

"Barbie's told me all about Gynedia and Queen Lilith and how the women select the men for their mates. Someday we'll be in charge in *this* world too," said Olivia.

"I don't care what Raggedy Ann here has told you about her make-believe universe. Now that I'm back, Barbie will be too busy doing her chores to have time for small talk. You don't talk to Jimmy about all this crap, do you?" asked Chip.

"We're taking a break from our relationship right now." Olivia teared up.

"See, what did I just say? Even a moron like Jimmy doesn't like that women's lib crap."

Olivia got up from the table and headed to her room. "Well, you could at least excuse yourself," he snapped. Barbie glowered at Chip, and Chip glowered at the last meatball on his plate.

"Why can't she be like my mother? She spent her day ironing my Dad's shirts and cooking his meals, trying to anticipate his every need. She never complained one day in her life about his drinking or his temper. She was a saint, that woman."

"But how can a woman love a man, if she's not happy and confident herself? She's dumped Jimmy, and she's enrolled in college. Jessica has offered to pay half her tuition for the first semester and maybe the whole thing if she does well. You need to cut her some slack, Chip."

Chip didn't need a scolding from the planet fairy. He finished the meatball, slurped up the remaining strings of spaghetti, and pulled another beer from the refrigerator, before wolfing down the raspberry pie that Olivia had made for his homecoming.

↬

The next day, Slobotnick met Chip for coffee. "I got an email from Pinky vid instructions."

"Instructions?"

"About the Barbie, as you call her."

"She's a wonderful slave, except for these ideas that she's putting in my daughter's head."

"That's exactly it. Pinky's email says ve need to get rid of her." He made a cutting motion across his throat. "Believe me, this von't turn out vell. Once the Lilith voman vill get a toehold, only God knows vat vill happen to your daughter and to this vorld."

"Toehold?"

"They vant to tell us vat to do, boss us around. They'll dominate good old red-blooded Jewish men."

"But I'm not…"

"Ok, *all* men, then. You vant a voman for a president, a voman car mechanic, or a voman defensive tackle? You vant to take orders, cook and vacuum, take out a garbage and clean a toilet vid Lysol tvice a veek. She'll sit on her lovely ass vhile you scrub shit from the bowl. Mark my vords."

"Hey, I'm not going to let any machine bully me, particularly a female machine."

"Chip, you'll be no match for her, believe me. Ve'll haf to turn her back to clay, or Mississippi mud, as you call it. In 1878 ve had a deadline, our golem vas digging ditches in Bohemia for the Emperor. Sure, maybe ve overvorked this guy a bit, but then this voman showed up, called herself Sabrina then, and she took him away. Our operation can't vork vid her around."

"You keep talking about an operation? What operation?"

"Ve steal from *schleppers* like Moskowitz, maybe a candlestick, a watch, or a necklace, could be a set of golf clubs. The golems do vork for people, it can't all be for free." Slobotnick pulled out a toothpick and picked at his rotten incisors.

"I thought golems were good for Jews, the blood libel and all that."

"That vas then, this is now. Yossel vorks for us now."

"Us?"

"Pinky and myself and a few others, some might call us devils," Slobotnick snickered. "Hey, just businessmen trying to earn a living. But ve can't do our business vid a snitch like Barbie or vatever her name is. Hey, if you hadn't insisted on a voman, ve'd have gotten a real golem and this vouldn't have happened."

"So now what?"

"Ve'll get her in a circle of fire, valk in reverse, and chant Pinky's chants that he sent to me, then she's dirt again."

"How do we get her in *the circle*?"

"Yossel."

"Yossel?"

"Ve'll redecorate him a bit, make him look strong and smart just like an Adam. She'll get the hots for him, like Lilith had for Mr. First Man."

"She'll fall for that?"

"Pinky guarantees it vill vork. Get Yossel over to your house for a marshmallow roast, and I'll take it from there."

"What if I don't want to be part of this scheme? Maybe I want to keep Barbie around for a while?"

"Ve'll cut you in on the haul that ve get from this trip. How about von million dollars? You'll never have to vork again, you vill be a rich man, Chip."

"Yossel brings in that much?"

"Actually, there's a thousand Yossels out there. Ve have them in homes, factories, and in the field picking strawberries and vhat not. Some look like businessmen, or craftsmen, or bank tellers, and some look like a Yossel. Novone misses a few tchotchkes here and there, and it adds up. Ve could make you a partner, a gentile like you could expand the business. Ve'll introduce you to some vomen who'll vant to be your friend, and vid them you can get a little rough if you vant. Ve'll even give you a new golem every year, guaranteed." Slobotnick grinned.

"I'll have to think about it."

"Here's an advance, vether you go through vid it, or not." The rabbi opened his briefcase and pulled out a bundle of cash. He counted out five crisp, one-hundred-dollar bills and gave them to Chip. "The rest is in here after ve do the job." He pointed to the briefcase.

⌒

Chip took Barbie and Olivia out for dinner that evening, to McDonalds. He munched on his Big Mac and fries, while the girls ate more greens, *goddamned salads at McDonalds*, he thought. He told them about the other truckers he'd worked with in Alaska. Bobby Chewbowsky, nicknamed "Chewy" with a tobacco plug in his mouth and always spitting, big-bellied Armando Hernandez, and a guy they called Glass Ass from sitting so many hours in his truck. He had to admit, Olivia was happier than he'd ever seen her, and beautiful Barbie caused his heart to skip beats up in his throat.

After dinner, Olivia went out with her girlfriends, while Chip watched a Cardinals game on TV. He began to shout epithets when the visitors scored four times in the first inning, causing Buster to retreat to his doggie bed in the kitchen. Barbie came over and sat next to him. Her scent was titillating.

"I saw the way Olivia looked at you tonight, she's a great kid, she really loves her Dad."

"Thanks for saying that, even if it isn't one hundred per cent true."

"It is one hundred per cent true. Us Gynedians know what we're talking about."

"Is it true that your mother was once Adam's lover?"

"We're all Adam's lover. Lilith had one thousand daughters, I'm just one of them." Chip fixed on her soft lips and artificially white teeth, as she smiled. Suddenly, he was pushing her down on the sofa, forcing his tongue into her mouth. The next moment, he was on the floor under the coffee table. He had a sensation in his lower gut as if his testicles had been squashed in a nutcracker.

"Goddamn, you came on to *me*," snarled Chip. "All I wanted was to have a good time."

Chip spent a restless night. He dreamed of Barbie tied down in his bed, her arms and legs lashed to the bedposts.

He wielded a serrated kitchen knife as she begged for
mercy. Then there was a baby in her arms, and the woman
who'd been Barbie was his mother. He watched from afar,
as the baby suckled at his mother's breast.

～

The next morning, Chip made breakfast for Olivia
before she left for work. He lingered over his second cup of
coffee thinking about the money Slobotnick had offered.
Barbie appeared in the kitchen. Her face was downcast,
and the tricycle tracks on her face were visible without
makeup.

"I guess I messed up last night," he said.

"You've got a lot of anger, Chip."

"Do I?"

"Have you considered therapy?"

"Yeah, Sigmund Freud." Chip laughed derisively.

"Lilith wants me back in Gynedia."

"And guess what? Slobotnick is evicting you sooner
than you think. We're planning a marshmallow roast.
Yossel will entice you to my fire pit, the rabbi will say
some new prayers, and poof you'll be gone."

"Yossel will *entice* me?"

"Yes. You won't be able to resist him."

"Let me guess, he'll look like the original Adam, and
I'll fall madly in love like my mother did eons ago. Sure,
I'll play along, and if Slobotnick screws up again, I just
might stay awhile longer." She laughed.

"Don't do me any favors."

"We could work on your hang-ups, and maybe make a man of you, a real man."

⌒

That evening, Chip lit the barbecue while Barbie prepared the potato salad and coleslaw. Slobotnick showed up in his white robe, carrying his briefcase.

Barbie greeted the rabbi. "Well, if isn't old Slobberpuss."

"You vere Sabrina vonce?"

"Yes."

"Ya, you vere taller, and your tits vere bigger, and you destroyed my golem."

"I saved that poor soul. Jacob wouldn't have survived, working in those conditions. He's now a prosperous silversmith in Gynedia."

"Gynedia, Shmynedia. Vid the right kind of clay, you'd never have come back here looking like something they sell in Toys R Us before Amazon put them out of business!" He crowed, as a bit of saliva shot through his yellowed teeth.

Ellen arrived with the dessert, along with Manny and Yossel. "I didn't know you'd be here, Rabbi. I just took these out of the oven."

"Vhat vould life be vidout a beautiful voman vid a delicious food," complimented Slobotnick as he grabbed a brownie from her plate.

"Will you be saying the blessings tonight?" she asked.

"Yes, and I have some special melodies too. Chip is interested in Judaism and I vant to acquaint him vid our traditions. I brought some books for him to study." He pointed to his briefcase and gave Chip a sly wink.

After the Sabbath prayers, Chip grilled one package of kosher franks and then another. Between Manny, Yossel and the rabbi, it looked like a Nathan's hot dog eating contest. Buster camped under the picnic table gobbling up crumbs.

After all the food was gone, the rabbi got up from his seat and cleared his throat loudly. "And now I vould like to announce the evening's entertainment... my beautiful singing voice and Yossel's magnificent prancing." Slobotnick began to chant in a low basso voice as Yossel arose from the table and started to dance, and as he danced, he transformed from a golem to a supple handsome man.

"Adam, what are you doing here?" cried Barbie.

Yossel grabbed Barbie in a clumsy embrace. "I love you, and I want to go away with you forever," he announced in a deep voice. He puckered up and found her unyielding lips, as they circumnavigated the firepit.

"Yossel will be leaving?" asked Manny.

"Ve got a lot more golems who could do a job, plus it's time for his tuneup," answered Slobotnick.

Olivia emerged from the kitchen with a large plastic bag and some roasting sticks. "How can we have a marshmallow roast without marshmallows? I even bought kosher ones."

But as she approached the dancers, there was a shifting of the earth's crust, accompanied by a concussive blast that scattered the guests, kicking up dust and debris like a

Saturn rocket launch. Chip hung on to the old dogwood for cover, while the poor dachshund, rolling like a log, bounced off the chain-link fence. Chip remained face down in the grass for several minutes until the tremor subsided, then he and the dog limped toward the house. A deep chasm had formed where the firepit had once been. Chip saw the Barbie doll lying unscathed near the edge of the crevasse.

Ellen and Manny appeared; their faces blackened with dust. "Shouldn't we call the police?" asked Ellen.

"And report what?" replied Manny. "That there was an earthquake in Chip's backyard? That we've lost a golem and a fairy, along with a bowling ball from our hall closet, and a bracelet from your jewelry box?"

"Where's Olivia?" asked Ellen anxiously.

Manny looked around. "This is none of our business," he said curtly. He grabbed Ellen's arm and pulled her toward their house.

Slobotnick materialized from the shadows, his white suit covered with dirt, like a ballplayer's home uniform after a belly slide.

"Olivia's with them, isn't she?" wailed Chip.

"Vhat did you expect for a million bucks?" answered the rabbi as he handed Chip the briefcase, then he and the BMW disappeared.

᷎

Chip picked up the doll and trudged back to the house. He sat down at the kitchen table and put his head on his truck-driver arms. *What an unlucky shit he was!* He looked up at the empty staircase leading to Olivia's bedroom. *All he ever wanted was some respect, some god damned respect.* He put his head back down and sobbed.

But then he thought: *She'll be so much happier in Gynie Land. She'll have a PhD in God knows what: women's psychology, women's zoology, women's history, women's studies of men. She'll have five male slaves and they'll cook and clean and wash and probably bear children for her. Barbie will be her wife and Yossel will be the best man at their wedding.*

"And I'll be free," he rasped, "I'll be fucking free." A tiny smile crossed his face as he glanced over at the briefcase. "And I'll be rich, free and rich. Jessica will mourn Olivia. It will serve her right for abandoning us, and I won't need her bitching or her money, and I won't need to fill Olivia's car with gas, or pick up after her, or take her dog to the vet, or spend twenty-five minutes cooking old-fashioned rolled oats for her breakfast. I'll buy my own robots who'll work for me!" he shouted.

He pushed his chair back noisily and reached for the wall phone. *He'd call Sally and announce that he was quitting the job. No more work for him!*

But then he replaced the phone in its cradle and dropped his head in his hands. "Oh my God, what have I done?" he whispered.

There was a thumping down the staircase, and Olivia appeared. Band-Aids covered her face and arms.

"Olivia? What happened? I thought you were..."

"The force pushed me down, and I fell face first on the patio. The next thing I remember, I was back in my bedroom. I must have fallen asleep until I heard you shouting and the chair scraping."

"I thought the golems took you."

"Barbie told me that Lilith was coming to rescue her. She said there was no chance that Slobotnick could get her back without Lilith's help, something about not knowing the spirit that was in my doll. I begged to go with her, but she said my place was here with you," she picked up the figurine from the kitchen table, "and the real Barbie."

She noticed the scuffed valise on the floor. "Hey, Rabbi Slobotnick left his briefcase here."

"He left us a special present, a very special present." Chip couldn't hide a sly grin.

Olivia opened the briefcase. "There's only some musty books in here. Here's one with a bookmark." She pulled it out.

Chip grabbed the valise and rummaged through it. "I was hoping for something more. Slobotnick promised me..."

Olivia opened the book at the marked page, and began to read. *Keep me as the apple of Your eye, and hide me under the shadow of Your wings.*

"Barbie told me to take care of you," said Chip.

"She told me the same thing."

"She did?"

"And that we needed to love each other." Olivia came over to Chip and embraced him.

"Can I start by making you dinner tomorrow?" Chip asked.

"Sure."

"Steak and potatoes?"

"Sure."

"With Brussel sprouts?" asked Chip.

"My favorite," said Olivia.

The Words of the Angel

My official name was Issur, and that's what they called me, Issur Plonk, but my Hebrew name was Itzhak, which translates to Isaac. And yes, you must be familiar with the biblical story; it doesn't matter if you're a Jew, a Christian, a Muslim or an atheist: God talks to Abraham one day and commands him to sacrifice his son Isaac. So too, in the shtetl of Pavoloch, a man named Avrum had that same dream. I was his only son, a fidgety nine-year-old kid who couldn't stop talking or making silly faces, who couldn't remain still long enough to learn his lessons. In a more recent century, it might be called attention deficit disorder, but in 1893, I was just a pain-in-the-ass disappointment to my father.

We lived on a meager piece of scruffy land that Papa rented from the Polish landowner. I helped my mother raise some chickens and sell some eggs, keep some goats and make some cheese. Papa didn't contribute to the chores. He spent most of his day studying the Bible and giving orders to my mother, Meeril. He considered himself a religious scholar and reserved the title *rabbi* for himself, even though there wasn't a building, a congregation or a following of bearded men to venerate him.

Like most Jews of that time and place, my father believed in a single, all-powerful god, known to the Jews as Yahweh, who had created the sun, the moon, the trees, the animals, and Man. He thought that Adam and Eve could have lived in paradise forever, if they hadn't sinned and ate of the sacred fruit. From then on, Man earned his living by the sweat of his brow, while Woman suffered the pain of childbirth and abject submission to her husband. The faithful Abraham became the first Jew, and Yahweh selected his descendants to be the Chosen People. Papa fervently hoped that one day this powerful god would test him, just as He'd tested Abraham.

He tried to teach me the sacred texts that so absorbed him, and he raised his voice in anger when my mind wandered from goats to chickens to flies to worms, and then there was the day that I left the gate to the chicken coop open, and a fox ate four hens which was a goodly part of our livelihood. Papa went berserk, and despite the screaming and pleading from my mother, he beat me with a leather belt on my naked behind until it bled.

∽

Rabbi Avrum Plonk woke up one fine morning in the springtime. He put on his tallis, his phylacteries, and his yarmulke, before reciting his prayers. Issur was feeding the animals, and Meeril was hunched over the old wood stove when Plonk sat down to await his breakfast. He drummed his fingers impatiently on the dilapidated table until his wife delivered a steaming bowl of buckwheat kasha with cinnamon sprinkles, along with two boiled eggs from the surviving hens. He chewed solemnly and deliberately, his bushy eyebrows unmoving below his wrinkled forehead.

After completing his last swallow, he asked, "Well Meeril, do you have anything to say to me today?" He said this when *he* had something important to say, but always started by asking her first. Unlike some Jewish men, he didn't make up for his lack of affection with self-deprecating humor.

"Why nothing Avrum, I have nothing to say, except to talk of the borscht that I'll be cooking for you. I'll be taking a trip to the market to buy carrots and beets and spinach and maybe a brisket if there was a slaughter today." She kept things simple and straightforward to avoid sarcastic comments from her husband. In Avrum's mind, if you knew the Bible and studied the great rabbis of the Talmud like he did, there was nothing left to know in the world, so that a wife like Meeril was not in a category to know anything about anything worth knowing.

After a pause, Avrum announced. "I had a dream last night." Meeril frowned slightly, because his dreams didn't usually turn out so well.

"And?"

"God spoke to my soul, and when God speaks to a Jewish soul, he belongs in the company of angels."

"Oh?"

"He had some advice. *Take now thy son, Isaac, whom thou lovest, and get thee into the land of Moriah; and offer him there for a burnt offering upon one of the mountains.* That's what he said, straight from Genesis 22."

Meeril turned white, her lips quivered, and she uttered an involuntary chirp like an injured chick that had fallen from its nest. "What are you talking Avrum?"

"Issur and I will be taking a journey."

"A journey, to Mt. Moriah?" asked Meeril.

"No, not to Mt. Moriah, just a walk in the forest and then to climb a hill, a few miles from Skivapolie. After that, we'll listen to hear if the Almighty has a few more words for us." Meeril stared down at her bowl of porridge. She had no saliva with which to eat. "Or maybe, just one more time, Issur can explain to me why he opened the door of the chicken coop to let the fox in."

"He's a little boy Avrum, just a little boy. Maybe he's forgetful, maybe not so brilliant as you would wish, maybe not so handsome, but he's our only son. A gift from God."

"Then let me be honest, Meeril. He's a poor student, full of silly questions that no one can answer. God has heard enough from our son, and He's greatly disappointed. Maybe Issur needs the fear of God in him." With this, Avrum smiled and Meeril fixed again on her cold breakfast. Avrum didn't often smile, and he didn't make jokes.

The next day, Avrum borrowed a mule from his neighbor along with a farm-hand, a Gentile named Gregory, who saddled the animal and loaded it with a stack of fire wood. Avrum called to Issur who was cleaning the chicken coop. "Come Issur, we're going on a little trip, to Skivapolie. We'll stay overnight at the inn and return tomorrow. On the way back, there's an ice cream shop in

the marketplace that makes the best ice cream in all of the
province of Kiev."

An hour into the journey, Issur began to complain.
"Papa my feet are sore, could I ride the mule, please?"

"No son, there's no room on the mule for you."

"But why is the mule carrying wood? If he didn't have
all that wood, I could ride on him."

"If there's a chill during the night, we'll need to start
a fire."

"But Papa, you told me that we'd take a room at the
inn in Skivapolie."

"I did, but if the rooms are full, we will need to sleep
outside."

The little group plodded on through the forest and
finally to the foot of the hill. Avrum told the attendant to
stay with the mule as he and Issur climbed to the summit.
"Papa why are you taking the wood with you?"

"We'll be praying at the top, and it could get cold up
there." When they reached the summit, Avrum placed the
wood on a large flat rock and instructed Issur to lie down
on it.

"What happens now?" The voice of little Issur began
to tremble with fear.

"We'll wait to hear the word of God," said Avrum, and
he raised his arms to the Heavens. Issur noticed a knife
tucked between Avrum's punishing belt and his shirt.

"Why do you carry a knife Papa?"

"In case we're accosted by thieves, Issur."

"But Papa, I don't want to lie here, and I'm getting
cold." The boy's eyes bulged with fear.

"Here son, I have a sweet drink that I brought with me. This will keep you warm." Issur drank it and fell into a deep sleep.

Avrum listened intently for the voice of the Angel of the Lord, the voice that had spoked to Abraham, but he heard only the wind as it whistled through the treetops. He watched the clouds scurry through the sky, as if anxious to get home before dark. He took the knife from his pants, and it gleamed in the sun's last rays. Soon twilight, then darkness came, as Avrum sat with his sleeping son.

ᕲ

And there I was, asleep on the funeral pyre, dreaming that I was at the famous academy of Shem and Eber, the son and great-grandson of Noah, reading the Bible and interpreting the words and phrases of the most difficult passages. I must have slept all through the night and into the early morning.

I awoke, shivering cold, with my hands and feet each bound together. I saw my Papa, sitting next to the rock with the knife in his lap, still awaiting instructions. But there was nothing, nothing but the eerie lament of a cuckoo, and the buzzing of bees beginning their day.

Finally, my sour-faced father untied me, and we walked silently down the mountain to where Gregory was waiting. We left the wood on the ground, and I rode back to Pavoloch on the mule. We didn't stop in Skivapolie for the ice cream that Papa had promised.

It was only later that my mother recited the angel's words to me, words that Papa desperately wanted to hear, words that would have made him Abraham's equal: *Lay not thine hand upon the lad, neither do thou anything to him.* But then again, he didn't kill me either.

The next year, 1893, my mother and I emigrated to Canada.

Ruthie the Dinosaur Eats the Forbidden Fruit

I was created by God, even though it's not clear if I was begat with the sea monsters on the fourth day or the quadrupeds on the fifth day, for there is no specific mention of dinosaurs in the book of Genesis. In fact, my real name isn't Ruthie but a very long Hebrew appellation, yet that doesn't explain the absence of my personage in the Holy Scriptures. I'm a gentle beast, if you can use such a word with *beast*, not vicious like a Tyrannosaurus Rex, or coated with armor like a Stegosaurus, but I do have the ability to fly, albeit rather feebly. My species is the Mamasaur with soft eyes and a feathery skin. We're devoted to family life, not to mention a special ability to put food on the table. No fossils of my ancestors have ever been found, so you won't find my kin in any paleontology books.

I couldn't believe that I was actually living in the Garden of Eden. Well, not exactly in the hallowed plot itself, but in an adjacent gravelly section that looked more like an unpaved parking lot without the chain link fence. I built a comfortable nest of twigs and leaves that I scavenged from the heavenly acreage, and I set up a serviceable kitchen. There were no humans yet, just a bunch of newly minted creatures like me. A pony lived nearby, and there was a flock of Merino sheep that munched on the pristine grass of the Garden, for weeds had yet to be invented. A petite penguin and a feisty kangaroo would drop in for a coffee klatch, and in a very short time, I began to gain a reputation as quite the hostess. The atmosphere was peaceful, and I never witnessed even one menacing cloud in the firmament. Life was perfect!

You must already know that Herman, the serpent, had taken up residence in this paradise. He seemed like a decent chap at the time, but as it turned out, I wasn't a particularly good judge of character. He lived down by the river, mostly concerned with finding a willing female with which to fertilize a few hundred eggs. I left him alone except for a polite hello when our paths crossed.

The sixth day was a seminal period in the history of the world, for that's when Man came down from the heavens which had been fashioned on the second day. There was a rumor floating around that this fellow was to rule over the fish, the fowl, and the animals, no specific reference to the dinosaurs, but I got the picture; this guy was going to be our boss, long before the Me-Too movement. There was no puff of smoke or anything like that. The naked biped just appeared in the orchard.

Woman arrived after a surgical operation performed by God, using a part of the fellow's anatomy, and if I could be permitted to editorialize, the deity did an excellent job.

She looked to be about eighteen, lissome and graceful, with beautiful white teeth and a skin you could die for. Mr. Male ran over to the maiden, and while holding his side rather gingerly, began to escort her on a tour of the Garden. Even a girlie dinosaur like myself could see a glint in his eye from the get-go.

I'm a relatively curious being, so I flapped over to the couple as they were picking succulent oranges off a tree, for in the beginning, the trees were created with fruit already on the boughs. It was only the following year that they needed flowers and bees to produce things, but that's another story. I plopped down near the pair who were ogling each other. At first, they didn't notice a nosy dinosaur neighbor, but in a nurturing tone I said to them, "Hi, my name's Ruthie. How are you feeling after all that creation? Can I get you some water or juice?"

"Nope, doin' okay, except for a pain when I laugh. My name is Adam, and this here is Eve. We were just comparing notes, and it seems that where I've got a gadget dangling down in front, she has some curly moss. On her chest, I notice she's got some things like what's on that tree over yonder." He pointed to the tallest tree in the garden with shapely fruit growing high in the branches.

"That's the Tree of Knowledge," I replied. "The serpent claims it produces a very special crop, but I've never partaken of them. There's an abundance of nutritious fare around here. You can get a dozen peaches for next to nothing, the mangos are delicious, and the pineapples are sweeter than candy. An excellent stir-fry can be prepared with the cauliflower and broccoli growing just over yonder hill along with both green and purple cabbage, so you really don't need to consume any of those pulpy pears perched in that tree."

"Yeah, God already warned us about eating that stuff," responded Adam, "but thanks for your tip on the broccoli. If you'll excuse us, Eve and I have business to attend to." As he settled himself in the grass alongside the pulchritudinous wench, I couldn't help notice that his limp noodle now looked more like a construction pencil.

Just as I became airborne, I witnessed Herman angling toward them in the grass. A few hours later, there was a ladder against Woody Wisdom as we nicknamed the tall tree, and Eve was standing on the highest rung picking the fruit. Before long, the lovers were popping generous morsels into their mouths. They saw me aloft in the freshly minted azure sky and waved at me to come by, so I swooped on in and grasped a large hunk of the fruit in my jaws. The sample was fibrous, and not that sweet, more like a Bartlett pear that you might want to place in a brown bag and leave on the counter to ripen for a day or two, or maybe add to a smoothie.

Suddenly, there was a loud thunderclap, the sun disappeared, and a stiff wind came up. Then the furious voice of God could be heard. As I fluttered to my refuge, I could hear him scolding Adam. The poor fellow was gesticulating and pointing over to Eve as if it were all her fault, a custom which has perpetuated since Man has resided on this earth. God turned to the serpent slinking away in the grass, and began to cuss at him too, and when I heard the Almighty swearing, I veritably trembled.

A few days later, I breathed easier, as it appeared that God was unaware of my nibbling on the verboten gourd. I spied Adam and Eve strolling in the providential patch. He was wearing a dark blue suit, and she had on a blouse and a long skirt. I plummeted down beside them. "You guys are all gussied up. What's the occasion?" I queried in my softest dinosaur voice.

"I'm really not in the mood for small talk," sneered Eve. "I found out that Adam is not the man I thought he was. After we have sex, he jumps up, and abruptly leaves with that devil, the serpent. They eat some cherries, pick some blueberries, and shoot the bull with the other critters. They don't come back until nightfall, and then he wants more favors." A solitary tear started down her perfect cheek.

"She's never satisfied, always complaining," responded Adam. "Ever since God chastised us, I've carried a heavy burden to provide for her, particularly now that there's a little one on the way. The Almighty has decreed that I will have to plough the fields, sow the seeds and harvest the wheat, but at least I'll be the boss." A toothy grin came over his face.

I flapped back to my cozy abode, but it was there that I received the shock of my life. God was there waiting for me, and by the look on his face, it wasn't to borrow my recipe for cabbage casserole.

"Ruthie, I'm very disappointed. Thought you could fool God, did you? Get off scot-free while your friends have been punished."

"No, my Lord. It was foolish to listen to my colleagues. I'm honestly sorry for my mistake, but after all, it was only a piece of fruit and not so good-tasting."

"Unfortunately, Ruthie," answered God in a sententious voice, "if you'd had parents, you would know that *sorry isn't good enough*." I heard a rumble which appeared to come from the deified stomach.

"Maybe you're hungry God. Here, try some poppy-seed cake, freshly baked, and I'll put on a fresh pot of coffee. The cheese blintzes will be out of the oven in about fifteen minutes."

He partook of the cake, eating in large mouthfuls. "I must admit Ruthie, this is good, very good," and He emitted a satisfied belch.

"Perhaps I could cook for you and clean that throne of yours, and maybe just maybe, if things worked out between us, I could be more than a housekeeper. One day, you might make me a female in Eve's image, I'd wear a white dress and there'd be a ceremony… and then we could talk about earth and life."

"Unfortunately, Ruthie, that won't work for me. You've sinned. Dinosaurs will exist on this earth for many years, but then you will become extinct. The only evidence that you ever roamed the earth will be the bones dug up for display in museums, and toys made in your image for children's play. No one will ever know that you lived in the Garden of Eden, for your name will be expunged from the Bible."

There was a puff of smoke and God disappeared. I never saw the Supreme One again.

Not long after, there was a calamitous fire and then a flood. When the waters receded, all of the plants and trees were gone including the Tree of Knowledge. The entire area resembled the stony plot next door. My dinosaur colleagues never forgave my irresponsible ingestion, and we all left the place to go our own way in the world. Even big Rex departed looking for a swamp, and the last time I saw Adam, he was tilling the rocky soil in his shirtsleeves, with Eve walking behind, holding an infant in her arms.

Ruthie's Cabbage Casserole Recipe

Ingredients:
1 Medium-sized onion
1 Small head of cabbage
Salt, pepper garlic
1 can of condensed cream of mushroom soup
1/3 cup of light mayonnaise
1 cup of Manischewitz crushed Tam Tams Crackers
¾ cup of shredded cheddar cheese

Instructions:
Preheat oven to 350°
Chop onion and cabbage, place in saucepan and partially
cook for 10 minutes
Season with salt, pepper and garlic
Mix mayonnaise and mushroom soup in separate bowl
Transfer onion and cabbage to a baking dish
Smear mayonnaise mushroom mixture over cabbage and
onion
Sprinkle crackers and cheddar cheese on top
Bake for 30 minutes

God's Sabbatical

Yehuda Popkin was born in the village of Lask, Poland, near the town of Lodz. The year was 1533. His father, Mendel, was a rabbi who was neither brilliant nor charismatic, and the size of his congregation was modest. His mother, Rivka, had three children until she died giving birth to Yehuda. The bereft Mendel arranged for his infant son to feed on the left breast of Chava Ginsburg, their housecleaner, while Chava's infant daughter, Golda, occupied her right breast. Golda was a vigorous and voracious suckler, and at six months, she was almost twice the size of the rabbi's asthenic son.

Mendel soon found another wife, for even a mediocre rabbi was held in high esteem by the Jewish community. He married a buxom eighteen-year-old, Tzippa Cukerman, a daughter of a moneylender. She turned out to be remarkably fecund, and they had six healthy children together. The fertile Tzippa became the dominant Tzippa, and eventually, Mendel himself didn't know if he ever had an original thought when it came to his large family and its finances. As a consequence, he buried his nose deeper into the Talmud, trying to decipher the Jewish god, Yahweh, and his mysterious ways.

The young toddler didn't smile or make eye contact, and he didn't say a word until he was four years old. By then, it was obvious that something was terribly wrong with the boy. The local physicians were of no help, still believing Aristotle's writings that the heart was the seat of intelligence. In those days, every twist and turn of life was attributed to the mercy or the wrath of God, so that the inhabitants of Lask believed that the Almighty had frowned upon Yehuda and his family for reasons unknown, but it was something that prayer had been unable to fix, even the supplications of a rabbinical father. A vicious rumor began to circulate in the community that the boy was occupied by a dybbuk, a Jewish demon.

As Tzippa's family multiplied, she was determined to remove Rivka's offspring from the household, thus reserving Mendel's meager income for her own children. She married off Rivka's two daughters soon after they reached puberty, and an older brother, Shimon, was sent off to study in Krakow. This left only the strange, incoherent Yehuda, from the first wife's progeny.

The little boy's behavior became more bizarre as he reached six and seven years of age. He would scream and cry when he couldn't be understood, rocking back and forth and banging his head into walls, doors and even hot ovens. He was only calm when Chava came over to clean the Popkin house, bringing Golda with her. The two children would skip rope and ride on a bedraggled hobby horse that had once been Mendel's. Golda was able to decipher

Yehuda's shattered language and strange mannerisms, the boy even laughed in her presence, but when Chava and Golda returned to their hovel, Yehuda would go back to his temper tantrums: punching, thumping, stomping, and whomping, not to mention wailing, which resulted from the whippings of Tzippa.

Yehuda was an impossible student. He was expelled from cheder because of his disruptions and his learning disabilities, but partly for his own sake. The other pupils taunted the poor boy mercilessly, taking delight in bloodying his countenance with their fists and their boots. He took to aimlessly roving about the village. Sometimes Kaminski, the shopkeeper, would give him a small piece of chocolate and the boy might smile, until one day, he caught Yehuda with a whole bag of Kaminski's candy in his school satchel. At thirteen, Yehuda was just able to write his name and recite a few blessings, not enough to celebrate a Bar Mitzvah. But despite all this, Mendel was a loving parent and unlike Tzippa, he never laid a hand on the boy in punishment. During his destructive moods, the rabbi would take him on walks and sing Jewish melodies to him, trying to calm the turmoil in the boy's psyche. Perhaps his black curly hair and pale complexion reminded him of Rivka, who in death evoked the image of Ruth or Esther compared to the dictatorial Tzippa.

The number of congregants dwindled as stories persisted that Rabbi Popkin was harboring a devil in his household. With his reputation at risk and the synagogue in dire financial straits, the despairing rabbi went along with Tzippa (did he have a choice?) and agreed to consign

Yehuda to a gruff dairyman who took the boy in exchange
for the forgiveness of a debt owed to Tzippa's father.

The farmer treated the boy like a slave. Yehuda was
awakened before the sun rose to help with the milking. He
was given a bowl of thin gruel before he led the cows and
goats to pasture. After that, he swept the barn, after that,
he brought the animals back from their grazing, after that,
he did some more milking, and after that, he ran away and
hid in Lodz where he eked out an existence as a beggar.
He wandered the streets, wearing a tallis and a yarmulke,
begging for a scrap of bread here, a cup of milk there,
an occasional egg, or a bowl of chicken soup. He became
thinner by the day and gave up speaking completely. He
would nod his head and take the crumbs that were given
to him. Sometimes he would offer himself to work as a
day laborer, cleaning out the stables of the rich men of
Lodz. He attended the services on Shabbos and the High
Holidays, but he reeked so badly of horse manure that the
sexton of the synagogue hid him in a dusty broom closet
where he prayed in silence, just barely hearing the chants
of the lusty cantor.

One day, while out begging, he fell in behind a wedding
party. He couldn't help but notice the bride in her dazzling
white wedding gown. As he ran up beside the nuptial
wagon, he recognized the bride as Golda, his breast-mate
from long ago. He waved his arms, his gaze fixed on her
angelic beauty, until he stumbled into a pothole, half-filled
with muddy rain-water.

When Yehuda was twenty-seven years old, he developed
a dry hacking cough, the harbinger of tuberculosis. His

meager appetite diminished even further, and he looked like a walking cadaver with a long straggly beard. One cold, snow-blinding day, he sought cover under a bridge and went to sleep. The following spring, as the snow was melting, a peddler noticed a foul odor as he was crossing that span. He notified the authorities, and Yehuda's decomposed body was found wrapped in his tallis. He'd been dead for four months.

It took several weeks for the body to be identified and transported to Lask. He was buried in the family plot next to Rivka and the fresh grave of Mendel who had died a few months previously. The family sat shiva for seven days, and his brother, Shimon, said the daily kaddish prayers for the required eleven months. A year later, a tombstone was unveiled over his grave with an epitaph in Hebrew, *He was a Man of God,* meant to dispel the notion that he was occupied by a devil.

Yehuda's spirit arrived in Sheol, the holding area for the Jewish dead, well before his body had been buried. He was so insignificant in life that an apprentice angel, working the night shift, was assigned to categorize his soul. Boguslaw had seen him coming, but it was almost dawn, and he was just starting in on his breakfast of kippered herring and rye bread smeared with goat cheese. Unlike souls, some angels were allowed to eat, and some of these beings had enormous appetites. The poor man was kept waiting in death as he had been in life. Finally, Boguslaw whispered. "Yehuda."

"That is I."

"You've just died, Yehuda."

"I knew I wasn't feeling well, but *died* you say?"

"Yes sir. I'm responsible for categorizing your soul and making sure it gets to where it needs to go."

"Well, Heaven, of course. For the torture that I led on earth, surely there must be a just reward for me in the afterworld. Isn't that how it works? We suffer on earth to get payback in eternity."

"Yes, in theory. But nowadays, there's a lot of red tape." Boguslaw remarked.

"Red tape?"

"Rules and laws and proclamations and edicts and decrees, stuff like that. Oh sure, some special ones come through here from time to time, big-shot rabbis, prophets, and rich people. The gentiles, of course, have kings and nobleman, queens and princesses, but I don't deal with them, I'm just here for poor Jewish souls like you. Other than your suffering, there's nothing that makes you qualify for a place in Heaven. No charitable deeds like giving money, food, or shelter to the poor."

"I *was* the poor. I was a beggar."

"Begging's nothing to brag about. You haven't prayed three times each day or fasted on Yom Kippur."

"I fasted daily. There was never enough to eat."

"That doesn't count." Boguslaw was getting edgy. "But Hell is another matter. You're not substantial enough for that."

"Substantial?"

"Well, you stole that bag of candy from Kaminski when you were a kid, and then there were the seventeen apples and eight pears that you pilfered from Goldstein's fruit stand over the years. But that's not enough to get you into Hell."

"So where to?"

"You're classified as *surplus*, a so-so soul, if I could use an alliteration." Boguslaw smiled at his witticism. "You're neither good nor bad. In fact, well over 70% of spirits fall into that category. As the earth's population has lived and died, there's been overcrowding. We can only store so many souls in Heaven, or Hell for that matter. You'll become a ghost and wander the earth until an opening comes up. Eventually you'll be recycled back into a living thing, could be a human, could be an animal of some sort, but that's above my pay grade."

"And the dybbuk?"

"Don't concern yourself with foolish superstitions. We're here in the real hereafter, no make-believe demons like that." Boguslaw chuckled.

"Wait just one minute, Mr. Angel, what about God?"

"What about Him?"

"What about His mercy, His kindness, and the rewards of one's devotion to the Supreme Being? He must realize there's been a mistake, and I can still get to Heaven for the tortuous life I endured, dybbuk or no dybbuk. Yehuda started to chant the sacred words, *"Shema Yisrael Adonai Eloheinu Adonai Echad.* Hear, O Israel, the Lord our God, the Lord is One."

"Unfortunately, God can't hear you right now. He's far away, working on other projects."

"Other projects?"

"The universe is constantly expanding. He has plans for creating new worlds, new heavens and hells, and performing miracles, stuff like that."

"What about here on earth with us Jews, the Chosen People and all."

"To be honest, He's evaluating other people in other galaxies. He let evil get into this world with that snake in the Garden, and things just got out of hand. Let's face it, everything's gone a bit haywire."

"Haywire?"

"Just look at yourself. Such a poor excuse for a human being."

Yehuda-soul was released into the biosphere. It had no form, no name, and no need for sustenance or sleep. It couldn't stop a runaway carriage, save a drowning child, furnish the needy, or minister to the dying. It couldn't even haunt a house. It travelled in the clouds, but couldn't feel the wind in its hair or the rain on its back. It didn't make an imprint in the sand or a ripple on water. Other apparitions passed by, middling souls like itself, and occasionally, they'd nod their heads in recognition. There could be fifty or more of these specters perched on a rock, on a dock, or in a sock. Yehuda-soul was blown all over the earth and back and forth in time. It viewed Stonehenge before the Druids, visited the Grand Canyon with the Paiute tribe, and frolicked amongst the Neanderthals, just another haywire scheme, it guessed.

It spent time hovering over Yehuda's grave. Once or twice, Shimon came by with his sisters, Gitel and Ella, and they placed stones on top of his tombstone in the Jewish tradition. After thirty years, it saw a grave dug and Tzippa's body was dropped in. Fifty years passed. It witnessed Golda's funeral, and it would have wept if a soul could cry. After seventy-five years, all its half-brothers and sisters were buried, and after a hundred, all their offspring were interred too. Eventually, no one even knew who Yehuda Popkin had ever been, although he hadn't ever been much. With the passage of time, his name and epitaph were eroded from his tombstone until it was a smooth gray tablet. Then, the soul stopped visiting. It found solace in the environs of a Manitoba forest, and lived quietly in a spruce tree with the squirrels.

In 1903, it heard a summons and was transported back to Sheol. "Long time no see, Yehuda." It was Boguslaw.

"Exactly 343 years since I've been only just a soul. Nice wings Bogey, something new?"

"I received my promotion in 1900. It took seventy centuries, but I made it to a full-fledged angel."

"What do you want from me?" asked the soul.

"An opening has come up. We're going to store you for a while, and then send you back to earth."

"Store me?"

"I've a spot for you, on the fourth block of the fifth row, in the fifteenth section of Heaven."

"Heaven, that's great news!"

"Andy thinks something big is coming down, so we've expanded."

"Andy?"

"Andy runs heaven nowadays."

"Not God and the patriarchs?"

"Andy was promoted from a human to Chief Angel. Not many have accomplished this feat other than Elijah and Enoch who were shot right up from earth in their chariots. You could include Jesus in that group, but that's a story for the Gentiles. Andy's the go-to guy nowadays."

"How did Andy manage that?"

"As a man, he was in advertising, in New York City no less. His birth name was Avraham Abramowitz, but he changed his name to Andy Anderson after he left Poland."

"There was a Rabbi Avraham Abramowitz in Lodz."

"Yes, that would have been his great-great-great-great grandfather. That rabbi's dear soul is in Heaven, in a special space with a spa, and an amphitheater where the spirits pray with the big boys: Abraham, Isaac, Jacob, Moses and David. After Andy died, his soul was located in the VIP section as well. Andy befriended Moses, and one day, he pitched his idea for a special addition to Heaven, where souls could be stored more efficiently. Andy had proposed a similar project for mass-producing prefabricated homes while working on Madison Ave. Moses talked to Abraham who talked to Yahweh. They advanced Andy up the ladder in order to implement his ideas. Now he's in charge of the daily workings of Heaven, you know, like a chief operating officer."

"You learn something new every day," said the soul.

"If you'll just approve these papers, we'll get you situated in your new home. It's a bit cramped, but you'll only be housed there until you're sent back to earth, less than fifty years I'd guess."

"How big a space do I have?"

"It's five inches by five inches."

"That's small even for a ghost. I'm used to living in a tree that's 80 feet tall."

"Ghost, schmost, soon you'll be a man again, ready to conquer the world. Remember Andy's slogan, *mighty men from little souls can grow*."

∽

Yehuda-soul found its little home at the end of a long corridor and keyed in the eighteen-digit number on the door handle. There was a soft click and the door swung open. Yehuda-soul peered in. There was a miniature blue and white box attached to one wall, a tiny chair, and a small table with a single drawer. Yehuda-soul opened the drawer and found a microscopic scroll. As it unrolled the scroll, a voice in the box began to read. *In the beginning, God created the heavens and the earth.* The voice continued to read until all of Genesis had been recited. Yehuda-soul began to feel weary and put the scroll back in the miniscule drawer in the diminutive table. After a while, it opened the scroll again, and like clockwork, the intercom voice started to read. This might have gone on for days or years; it didn't know, there was no way to keep track of time. The soul didn't see the sun or the moon or the stars or the dancing aurora borealis during a Manitoba winter. It just existed.

One day, Yehuda-soul heard a rustling, like a sparrow outside. The pint-sized door swung open. A wispy being stood at the threshold. There was a beguiling softness to the ghost that Yehuda-soul remembered from the time it had been a man.

"This is my old apartment. There must be some mistake," said the satiny soul.

"Aren't you Golda?"

"Who?"

"Golda, Golda Ginsburg. I shared your mother's breasts with you when we were infants."

"When was that?"

"In 1533, when we lived in Lask, Poland. You were my playmate."

"I've lived many lives since then, I think five or six. Once I have a new body, I forget the flesh that came before. My last stop was Cincinnati. I was a teacher who taught in an orphanage. I had four wonderful children, and a fine husband, a doctor."

"I've never been human since I was Yehuda in Lask. I saw you on your wedding day, but you didn't recognize me."

"It wasn't to be, I guess."

"I couldn't talk or think properly as a man, and I ended up a beggar. After I died, I was classified as a surplus soul. I travelled the world as a phantom, then I lived in a tree for two hundred years. Now, I guess we'll share this little space. I've been so bored in here all by myself."

"It's different since Andy took over," said Golda. "We used to hold prayer meetings with all the souls. We'd sing and dance. David would play his lyre, and we'd praise God. Now we're packed in here like sardines, and they pipe that canned Bible into each cell. Andy says God's on sabbatical." Golda-soul emitted something like a sardonic laugh.

"Maybe this is God's will. For you to be my soulmate," said Yehuda-soul.

"You think?"

And so, they co-habitated in their tiny cell. Yehuda-soul would tell Golda-soul how hard his life was in Lask, and how much he loved her then. Golda described the gentleness of her husband, the delight of sixteen grandchildren, and her work with the orphans. They talked about what their life might be like on earth: the cities they would visit, the food they would eat, the anniversaries they'd share, and the love they would have for each other. Yehuda blushed, if a soul could blush, and told Golda that he'd never had sexual relations with a woman, but Golda told him he'd do just fine. But they never spoke of God, Golda wouldn't allow it. They communicated with Boguslaw, and begged him to return them to earth as a couple. They didn't care if they were rich or poor or where they lived. They knew that life could be hard, even cruel, but anything would be better than a cell five inches by five inches.

It was some twenty years later that Boguslaw spoke to them through the intercom. "I've been talking to Andy, and I've got good news. He thinks he can work things out for the two of you. You'll both be born in Europe next month, Yehuda in Prague and Golda in Vienna. You'll meet when you're twenty years old." The two souls began to sing the Shema. Yehuda-soul was surprised that Golda was singing.

Then Golda asked, "How did you get Andy to agree? I thought he'd abolished romance."

"He has, but he apologizes that you two ended up in the same cubicle. That isn't supposed to happen. He'll let you have your fun on earth, but there is a catch."

"Catch?" asked Yehuda-soul.

"He's not sure how many Jews he'll need in the future. Your next gig could be a new group of humans that he's designing. You might not be Jews the next time around. Andy's always tinkering."

"Where will we meet?" asked Golda-soul.

"In Poland, in Lodz, in the ghetto, in 1942."

"That's where I died as a beggar. Andy's got a sense of the theatrical," said Yehuda-soul. He laughed while wrapping his wisp even tighter around Golda's ethereal tendrils.

"Two years later, you'll travel to your final destination."

"And where would that be?" asked Yehuda-soul.

"I'm not sure he's worked that out yet," said Boguslaw.

The Pandemic in Pikov

A broken Pinhas Sapotskin shuffled along the main street of Pikov, a dusty shtetl on the Southern Bug River. Tears filled his sodden eyes, then spilled down onto the front of his fetid kaftan. In his grief, he wasn't conscious of the way he smelled, or the way he looked. His beard was long and straggly, the hairs in his large nose protruding; growths that had been lovingly snipped by his Laika over the course of their ten years of marriage. They didn't have children like the others, thank God, so she took care of him like a precious jewel, but in just three days she was gone, as the pandemic devasted the little town that had just recently been so prosperous.

Laika had taken ill with profuse vomiting, and then the diarrhea which went from brown to a dirty grey. She became prostrate and weak, filling the bed with her eliminations, begging unceasingly for drinking water which Sapotskin desperately drew from the well that served the poorer part of Pikov.

The Gentile doctor, Dr. Ivan Demchenko, was kind enough to attend to Laika and confirm the diagnosis.

The miasma, the vapor cloud of cholera, was spreading throughout all of Russia and the world. He prescribed the standard treatments of magnesium and castor oil, along with quinine, always the quinine, then he applied a mustard plaster and attached a dozen leeches to her skin to suck her blood, blood that she desperately needed to survive. He administered these feckless and mostly harmful treatments, then sadly announced to poor Sapotskin that his wife would most likely die before the dawn of the next day. After he left, Laika began screaming with abdominal cramps as the vital fluids poured out, then her pulse weakened and her lips turned blue. Her breathing halted and she became silent for eternity. A simple intravenous solution of salt water could have saved her life, but that was not to be. In 1850, only Dr. Demchenko's dire prediction of death made any medical sense.

And now Sapotskin, in his grief, was on his way to talk to Rabbi Chernovsky about funeral arrangements. He entered the small synagogue and waited outside the rabbi's study. He stared at the oak door as if his wife might be behind it, offering some of her cherry strudel, and laughing at the rabbi's stale drollery. A few minutes later, it opened, and his neighbor, Judah Levy, appeared in the doorway. The man could barely move, like a force had sucked him into the floor. His clothes hung on his scant frame as if on a ghost, his stoop carried the weight of the world, and the grief in his face told it all: a son and a daughter. "A mass burial today for ten bodies, can you believe it?" he said.

Sapotskin nodded his head. "I'm sorry for your loss dear friend. Such children."

"You too?" asked Levy.

"I've lost my Laika."

Just then he heard the high-pitched chirp of the diminutive rabbi from inside his sanctum. "Come in Pinhas."

"You've heard about my wife?"

"Her body arrived on a cart with nine others this morning, the sexton gave me a list of the dead. She'll be buried with the others before sundown."

"A few days ago, she was strong and healthy and singing and…"

"Yes, it's God's will."

"Is it?" asked Sapotskin. "Is it God's will, that's what God wanted? To take my wife away from me forever?" His voice cracked with sorrow as he pronounced that fateful last word.

"We can't explain everything about the Almighty. We have fifteen families who've lost loved ones, and they all ask the same questions."

"But not you, your children are at work, your grandchildren playing in their playground, your wife able to light the candles this evening. No, it's not you."

"By the grace of God, I don't know why Pinhas." *The rabbi is aware of my sins and blames me,* mused Sapotskin. He'd attended synagogue on most days to pray, most days except when it was raining or cold or snowy. And maybe the rabbi even knew about the smoked pork loins that he consumed in Kiev with the Gentile merchants, and the other Gentile loins that he had partaken of from time to time in his youth. Then there was the drinking in the tavern on some Sundays, and placing bets with Chezik, the gambler.

"So, that's all you can tell me? It's God's will, but you don't know why. Over a hundred inhabitants of Pikov have already perished. Have we all sinned so outrageously?" whined the despondent Sapotskin, the tears once again flowing amongst the whiskers of his chin and cheeks. He pulled out a soiled handkerchief and wiped his face.

"God works in ways that we mere mortals can't know, we just can't." Chernovsky responded in the pious tone reserved for rabbis.

"How about Judah Levy? Such a religious man, a teacher and a scholar of Torah, why is he castigated by God? And what about Isaac Nemerovsky and Noah Berenboim and Yaacov Kamenetsky?" But then who knew what really went on in a man's mind, the lusting, the desires, the jealousy, the cravings. God knew the evil ones; He knew the sinners.

"We must pray, and God will comfort us in our time of need. Listen to me, that's the best anyone can do." There was an edge in the rabbi's voice, as if he was exasperated with Sapotskin's questions and maybe with God. The rabbi got up on his tippy toes and put his hands on the poor man's shoulders, then he recited the words from the Book of Psalms. *"Give thanks to the LORD, for He is good, His love endures forever."*

The rabbi might have had more praying to do, but at that moment, Sapotskin pulled away, and rushed out of the room. He slammed the door behind him, shaking the timber of the ancient synagogue. Some rabbi, some man of God, he thought. It's all about praying and praising the almighty, reciting a prayer and singing a song, but when something goes wrong, goes terribly wrong, where is He?

Where is an angel, a spirit, or even a saint? On his way home, he encountered Judah Levy sitting on a bench in the village square. He sat down beside him. There was silence between them.

"Why Judah? Why? Why so many dead?"

"It's Samael, the evil angel, the devil. He's taken over the town and the entire country of Russia. They say he brings the putrid air to the sinners."

"And the Gentiles who have sinned, they're included?" asked Sapotskin.

"I guess so."

"No help from Jesus or the Holy Spirit for them?"

"I guess not."

"And you, the purest man I know. Why you?"

"About five years ago, I didn't say my morning prayers. I slept too long after going to bed late that night. I forgot to say the blessing on the wine one Sabbath eve, and then there was the time that my wife found a few crumbs of bread in the house during the Passover."

"That's why He took your children? For crumbs?"

"That allowed the Angel Samael to poison the air." Sapotskin got up from the bench and patted the back of Levy's slumping figure.

He noticed his brother-in-law, Motel Zeiberling, leaving the bakery with a loaf of rye bread and a bag of rugelach (cinnamon rolls). Motel was a rich man, a merchant of fine wines and linens and precious gems. He lived high on a hill, in a large house on the outskirts of town. His wife and children were well.

"She died Motel."

"I know, Pinhas. The funeral will be later today."

"Why Motel? Why?"

"Having suffered on Earth, the merciful God will take care of my beloved sister. I know that to be true."

"They say that the Devil has taken over from God," said Sapotskin.

"He has the upper hand in this sickness, but the worse it is for us Jews on earth, the better things are in the world to come," answered Motel.

"But look at you, and your beautiful healthy family. Should they suffer more in the hereafter because of the prosperous life that you've provided for them?"

Motel placed his outstretched arms perpendicular to his body, bread in one hand, the rugelach in the other, and shrugged his shoulders up to his ears.

∽

The burial service was completed. The mourners recited the Kaddish for the dead, and lowered Laika and the others into their graves, then shoveled the earth over them to complete the finality of death. Sapotskin trudged home to his empty house. It wasn't long before he developed the excruciating symptoms of the dreaded disease. He lay in his bed and hoped he would die. For what was a life without his Laika?

He drifted into a fitful sleep, into the ether, the clouds, or his unconscious brain. Then there was a mirror, and in the mirror appeared a short man, his face barely visible above a large mahogany desk. In the background, there was a dark maroon wall adorned with a pattern of Jewish stars and yellow shofars, and Sapotskin realized it was a replica of the rabbi's study. The image spoke to Sapotskin in a high-pitched voice.

"How are you Pinchas, how are you bearing up in this time of travail and sadness?"

"Not well, not well. Did you know that you look and sound like Rabbi Chernovsky from Pikov?"

"I could come up with a different voice and visage, if you'd prefer."

Sapotskin couldn't repress a sob. "I hope you're taking me away to join my wife."

The creases on the spirit's forehead deepened. "That's an interesting question."

"It's not a question, it's a statement. But if not, why not?"

"It's not that simple."

"Such a wonderful woman, who could bake and clean and cut my hair, wherever it might grow. The greatest of angels, if you'll excuse the comparison, who would listen to all that a talkative Jewish man had to say even when he becomes boring, repeating the same story over and over, talking about this and that, and that and this, that he talked about the day before and will talk about the next day, the puns, and the aphorisms, or some fact that he read in some book or another, and the jokes, all the jokes. Did you ever hear about the cat with three legs?"

The apparition remained solemn. "Your wife's in a holding area. We call it Sheol, the Gentile's word for it is *limbo*. A few things have come up with her, I'm sorry to say."

"Well sure, she cursed, mostly at me, but it was a loving kind of swearing and she never meant it, and she swore at me with good reason, like when I didn't come home when I was drunk, or I lost money from my gambling. Please sir, throw all that stuff out and look into her soul."

"Your wife was somewhat of a thief, Pinchas."

"I know that. When we first got married, we were desperately poor, and she did the laundry for a rich family and every so often she would take some kopeks from the man's pants pocket, or the ladies' undergarments, or a fine agate from the little boy's marble collection…"

"She stole all of her life, Pinchas, even if it was small things, but stealing is stealing, it's one of the ten commandments."

"She kept no secrets from me. She'd go to the fairs in Berdichev and when the baker had his head in the oven, or the tchotchke seller turned his back to haggle with another customer, she'd take a few scones or a brooch and maybe a cheap ring, but we were not well off due to my drinking and gambling, and the grain business was up and down. There wasn't money for ornaments and trinkets, but I would laugh and she would laugh, and like you said, just small things."

"We can't have a stealer in heaven at least without some punishment, maybe her soul will enter an antelope or one of those cats that you make jokes about, but I can't guarantee a pass to heaven, Pinchas."

"But doesn't everyone have some good and bad in them? And believe me, there was more good in this woman than bad."

"Well sure, there's some bad in everyone, like your friend with the crumbs on Passover problem. That's why I brought the cholera pandemic, to punish the sinners."

"Wait a minute here. You're no angel, are you? You're the—"

"Let's put it this way, I'm a representative of misfortune."

"Where's God?

"He's around. He's having a tough time with all this cholera, believe me, it wasn't His idea, it was mine!" the gnome bounced up and down with glee. "But without Him, it could be worse, it can always be worse."

"Worse, it could be worse than this?" Sapotskin was tempted to break the mirror with his fist.

"You're sick now Pinchas, but you'll survive and live to an old age. Naturally, when the time comes for the final judgement, I'll put in my two cents, and I can't guarantee heaven, not with what I see so far. And why can't you get out of bed on a snowy day to attend services?"

"But I want to be with my wife, I want to die now. I'll be living in Hell here on earth, without her."

"All I can tell you Pinchas is that God works in strange ways, ways that can't always be understood even by the Devil himself. Then the little demon quoted from the bible, *"And, behold, the Lord passed by, and a great and strong wind rent the mountains, and broke in pieces the rocks before the Lord; but the Lord was not in the wind: and after the wind an earthquake; but the Lord was not in the earthquake: And after the earthquake a fire; but the Lord was not in the fire: and after the fire, a still small voice."*

〜

Sapotskin awoke. His fever had broken and his pain had eased. He heard the moaning of his neighbor next-door, and the wailing of the man's young daughter. Motel's wife came by with a large bucket of fresh water from their well, and he drank thirstily. She cleaned his bedroom and put fresh linens on the bed and cooked a few boiled eggs and made him eat. Slowly, he recovered from his illness. After a few days, he realized that he was among the living, but he wished he could have died, and he cursed himself again for being a sinner.

When half the town had been buried, the pandemic slowly lifted its grasp. Sapotskin recited the mourner's Kaddish for the required twelve months and prayed every day that a loving and caring woman such as Laika was in heaven. After a while, he sold his house and its memories, and moved in with the next-door neighbor, now a young widow, who had lost her husband and her only child in the pandemic. Eventually he married her, and he took over the small dry goods store that her husband had owned, and it prospered. Then to his surprise, they had a small son and then another, and then a daughter. Life and love went on in Pikov and in all the world.

Ten years later, Sapotskin noticed that a new well was being dug in the town, a mile from their old well and further away from the river. He walked over to investigate and found Dr. Demchenko observing the digging along with Judah Levy.

"Something wrong with the old well, doctor?" asked Sapotskin.

"Something was always wrong with that well, but we didn't know it," he replied.

"Yes, sometimes there was a bad taste to the water, and we couldn't drink from it," said Levy.

"It was contaminated with *kaka*," remarked the doctor.

"Well sure, we suspected that," said Sapotskin and they laughed.

"It was more than a joke," said Demchenko. "I just came back from Kiev where I heard a lecture by a renowned scientist, an Englishman, who's an expert on cholera. He believes that the disease is caused by contamination of the water supply. The old well is too close to the river where people dump their human waste. Some of that waste-water seeps into the well from the river and that's how cholera is spread. It has nothing to do with evil vapors in the air, it's not a miasma brought by the devil."

"Does that explain why the people on the high ground hardly got sick?" asked Sapotskin.

"Yes, they drank from a different well, a well that was much cleaner."

"So, the pandemic had nothing to do with sinning or punishment or the devil or a grand strategy of the almighty. God works in strange ways, if he works at all," said Sapotskin.

"Just bad luck," said the doctor.

"But then again, maybe God had all of the *unkoshers* live down by the river so that they'd get sick," said Levy.

Author's Note

There have been seven pandemics of cholera, and a recent outbreak in Yemen has killed over three thousand people. In 1884, Robert Koch discovered the cholera bacillus and proved that it was spread by contaminated water. In the 1890's, Waldemar Haffkine, a Jewish scientist from the Ukrainian shtetl of Berdiansk, developed a vaccine for cholera and was knighted by Queen Victoria for his discovery. He lived in India for many years, and saved millions of people with his vaccines for cholera and bubonic plague. The Haffkine Institute for Training, Research, and Testing still exists, and is affiliated with the University of Mumbai.

Two Goats and a Dog

It was a frigid Russian winter. It had been cold since the autumn of 1881, and now it was 1882. Rabbi Chaim Kitzes buttoned his threadbare coat over his yellowed tallis, placed his fur cap tightly over his yarmulke, and pulled on his sheepskin boots. He closed the door softly so as not to wake his wife, then trudged painstakingly through the snow-covered village of Babanochka, a shtetl whose exact location has been lost to history. He entered the small synagogue and stamped out the slush on his galoshes. The beadle, Berenshtein, had started a small blaze in the small fireplace in the small shabby room that served as an office.

"Very cold," said Berenshtein.

"Yes," said the rabbi, "I guess the others aren't here yet?"

"Do you see them?" Always that sarcastic attitude, thought Kitzes, but where to find another man who would work for so little? Just then the door opened and Rabbi Hirsh Mendel entered along with Rabbi Mordecai Schmelke. They'd taken a horse-drawn carriage from the nearby town of Usman where their more prosperous congregations were located. Berenshtein took their coats, and they sat down at the dilapidated oak table that doubled as Rabbi Kitzes' desk.

"When do the morning prayers begin?" asked Rabbi Schmelke.

"It's so cold, we might not get ten men for the minion today, plus we don't need the whole place to know our business right now," said Rabbi Kitzes. The others nodded their heads silently. Kitzes was right. This had to be kept quiet.

"Tell us about your dream," said Rabbi Mendel.

"He's *the one* according to the angel, the Chosen One for the Chosen People," smiled Kitzes.

"It's about time," said Mendel. "The people are reeling from the crop failures, outbreaks of cholera and smallpox, never mind the persecutions, the pogroms and the decrees by the Czar limiting our people's livelihoods. Just last week, three Jews in Posukevka were beaten to death by hoodlums."

"So, who's this fellow to get us out of our misery?" asked Rabbi Schmelke, trying to contain his excitement.

"He's a pious man from Shpola."

"Shpola? I don't remember any Talmudic scholars from around there," said Rabbi Mendel.

"Well you wouldn't. According to the Angel Tzadkiel, he's a shepherd with two white goats and a black dog. His name is Itzik."

"Itzik with two goats and a dog?" queried Berenshtein with a sour look.

"Is that enough to be a *Messiah*?" wondered Schmelke aloud.

"Shh," the other rabbis shushed him. Just saying the word brought shivers down their spines and cramps to their kishkes.

"Could we maybe get some clarification?" asked Rabbi Mendel.

"Clarification how?" asked Kitzes.

"Dream some more and the Almighty will clarify."

⤸

That very night, Rabbi Kitzes curled up beside his ample wife, Feiga. "You have herring breath, Chaim." Feiga was never one to pull any punches, particularly in regard to her husband and particularly in bed. She'd married a rabbi according to her parents' wishes and ended up with a man that couldn't rub two kopeks together to save his life. A man who had memorized the Torah, and studied with the great-great grandson of the 19th disciple of the great Baal Shem Tov of Medzhibozh. A husband who could argue Jewish ethics with the best minds in the shtetls of Poland, Russia and Lithuania, but a decent table to put food on, they didn't have, and with a faulty stove of thirty years, it was a miracle that she could produce her special chicken soup, or even a borscht for that matter.

"I needed energy for tonight, so a pickled fish, I ate."

"Energy for who, for what?"

"For the angel. He'll come tonight. He promised in two weeks and two weeks is up."

"Not this Messiah talk again?"

"What other hope do we Jews have?"

"Well, we could move to Odessa and you could work in my brother's bookbinding operation and still go to synagogue all you want. And we could have a house that's decent with some furniture with a flowery upholstery and..."

"I guarantee he's coming tonight." The rabbi rolled away from his wife, shut his eyes, and covered his ears until her muttering and burbling gradually faded. Then he was looking in a mirror. A portly apparition appeared. He wore a pointed black hat and a black fur-lined robe. His hands were soft and white, and his eyes twinkled behind rimless glasses.

"We've been working hard on getting him ready," the angel said.

"That so good to hear, Angel Tzadkiel." Rabbi Kitzes wished to talk face to face, but the spirit was only visible in a mirror. On the other hand, in a dream, face to face maybe wasn't all that important. "So, is it still the goatherder from Shpola? I was talking to my esteemed colleagues today, and they seem to think that this man might not be ready for such an important task. I mean, a lowly goatherder with two goats and a mongrel. Maybe he needs to start as a rabbi or a seer and work his way up to a prophet, maybe an angel like yourself, and then ..."

"He's the one, make no mistake."

"But how will he convince Jews from Zvenigorodka and Zlatopolie, never mind the world, that the End of Days is coming, when all the souls that ever lived will reawaken to live forever in the Garden of Eden?"

"Go visit the man and bring him to your house."

"Then what?" But the angel had disappeared from the mirror.

❦

The next day there was another snowstorm, and then another, and it was almost a month before the rabbis could negotiate the road to Shpola in a donkey cart. Berenshtein was in the driver's seat prodding and cursing King David, the mule, while the rabbis sat behind on a hard bench, trying not to hear the beadle's obscenities. They reached the outskirts of the village and encountered a tinker shuffling along with a heavy load of pots and pans. Rabbi Kitzes inquired about a man named Itzik with two goats and a dog. The man, without saying a word, pointed to a small track that veered off the main road.

Soon they stopped at a small cottage where some goats were grazing. A little black dog ran up to them barking hysterically, spooking poor King David, and it was all Berenshtein could do to rein him in. Itzik Gershkovich peeked out his door to see what the racket was about. The rabbis inhaled sharply when they saw him. He was a thin fellow with a greasy head of hair and unruly sidelocks. His head was large for his body, and it needed to be large, for it housed a nose with such a hook and nostrils, that it was impossible to visualize how air could make its way through the convoluted passages. He picked up the dog, who immediately stopped yelping, and came toward the wagon.

"Hello august men, I'm Itzik," he said in a squeaky voice.

"The Angel Tzadkiel came to me in a dream and declared that you were a special human being, maybe a superhuman being such as the Messiah," said Rabbi Kitzes with a nervous laugh.

"Yes, that's true," said Itzik. He put the dog down and the canine curled up at his feet. "The angel has told me to lead our people to Jerusalem to mark the End of Days."

"You *are* a pious man are you not?" asked the practical Rabbi Mendel.

"Pious for sure."

"Pious is pious!" exclaimed the effervescent rabbis.

Rabbi Schmelke asked, "Are you learned in the ways of the Torah?"

"I study as best I can, but being so poor I've not been able to learn from the feet of such scholarly men as you."

"So, might I ask, why did He pick *you*?" pursued Rabbi Schmelke.

"Why did He pick *me*?" repeated Itzik.

"Can you raise people from the dead, or split the Red Sea, or stop the sun in its orbit?" asked Rabbi Mendel. "You'll need something so people will follow you to the holy land and give up their earthly possessions."

"The angel never mentioned anything about miracles." Itzik stared down at the snow-covered ground.

"Then why a skinny Jew such as you, like a sack of bones who hasn't eaten for a month?" asked Mendel.

"I guess because I'm the most honest man that's existed since Moses or even Abraham." The rabbis recoiled in shock. *Honesty?* Surely there must be more to it than that, the angel must have consulted with God. "Well virtuous too, I've never sinned in my life."

Rabbi Mendel pondered his gambling addiction, Rabbi Schmelke ashamedly fondled a small bottle of vodka in his vest, and Rabbi Kitzes recollected the nubile Aleksandra, the nobleman's daughter, from long ago.

"And I know the sins of every Jew," said Itzik.

"What do you mean?" asked Kitzes.

"I know the sins of every Jew that every lived. That's the gift that God has given me. With your help, I'll visit all the shtetls in Russia, and I'll point out every person's transgressions. They'll repent, and I'll carry their burdens until they become as pure as I." The young man twitched his protuberant proboscis in solemnity.

The rabbis took their leave to the shabby inn in Shpola. There was little talk as they sat over a meal of cooked cabbage and boiled chicken feet, each thinking of their misdeeds to be revealed by the Messiah. They fervently recited the evening prayers, before tossing and turning in fitful sleep.

Angel Tzadkiel returned to Rabbi Kitzes. He had a cheery expression on his cherubic face. "Have you ever met a man more righteous?"

"Pious is pious," said Rabbi Kitzes.

"Plenty pious, for sure," said the angel.

"He needs to work on his Torah," said Kitzes.

"You will shelter his dog and his goats, and teach him Torah and Talmud until the snow melts. In the spring, he'll meet with your parishioners and reveal himself as the Messiah. This is God's will," said the angel.

The next day, Berenshtein loaded Itzik and the two goats and the dog onto the cart, and King David plodded with his heavy burden back to Babanochka.

↩

Thus, the goatherder and the rabbi commenced their study of the Jewish scriptures, embellished by Kitzes' stories about famous Hasidic rabbis that had lived in the Pale of Settlement for centuries. The Messiah proved himself to be an adequate student, if maybe not spectacular, and the studies were continuously interrupted when Itzik needed to milk the goats and feed the dog. He had to purchase fodder for the animals until springtime, and when the farmer down the road asked for payment, Itzik shrugged his shoulders, so that Rabbi Kitzes forked out his meager savings to cover the debt, while poor King David lost his appetite sharing his stall with the two bleating ungulates. Meanwhile, the little black dog ran all over the house, barking at the slightest noise, nipping at visitors, and producing excrement on the rabbinical rugs during the cold days when he refused to go outdoors.

One day, the goats chewed up the undergarments hanging on the clothesline, and Feiga had had enough. "This man you call the Messiah needs to leave," she announced one night as they lay in bed.

"How dear Feiga can I request this of such a blessed man."

"I can't live another day with him, in fact, going to Gehenna couldn't be much worse. If he was truly a messiah, he could produce the milk and cheese himself with no need of these stinking goats, plus there's nowhere in any teaching where the Messiah owns a dog. And why doesn't he know everything there is to know about Judaism without getting instruction from you?"

"Let me ask Tzadkiel what to do."

"Oh sure, go meet with your boyfriend, the angel."

That night, Tzadkiel radiated holy happiness. "Everything's going well, the Almighty has signed off on him."

"Signed off? I thought he was picked by God from birth."

"No, he's on a trial basis, and you're the trainer."

"His animals are a burden to us. My wife tells me that she would rather live in hell."

"Your wife blasphemes, Chaim. And just think, being his teacher, you'll be as famous as the Messiah himself." Rabbi Kitzes' audible snoring hushed as he reveled in the words of the angel. "Tomorrow, after the Sabbath services, proclaim the man from Shpola as the Messiah and have him give a speech. Soon after, the world will know of the great coming." Tzadkiel smiled as he faded from the mirror.

∽

At services the next day, the rabbi introduced Itzik, the goatherder, as the Messiah. There was a collective gasp, as the congregation realized that the large-nosed individual living with the rabbi was more than a maker of cheese. After the sighs of disbelief, the worshippers began to whisper amongst themselves, and soon they were singing and dancing in the aisles. Rabbi Kitzes shouted to maintain order as Itzik mounted the podium. The goatherder cleared his throat and began to speak in his high-pitched voice.

"I'm here today to announce my intention to be your Messiah, now and forever. Soon, the prophet Elijah will appear in Israel, and he will blow the ram's horn to herald my arrival. All the Jews in the world will gather in the holy land, and all the souls that ever lived will be raised from the dead, and the temple in Jerusalem will be rebuilt to its former glory." Huzzahs erupted throughout the congregation with kissing of husbands and wives and children and cousins and aunts. Even skeptical Berenshtein grabbed the synagogue's shofar and began to blow, first in a staccato rhythm and then in long sonorous notes.

When the congregation quieted, Itzik continued. "And one more thing, everyone will have to confess his sins to purify himself." The crowd resumed their jubilance. Women jumped up and down, their long dresses inching above their ankles, while toddlers sat on their fathers' shoulders and clapped their little hands. They would leave the pogroms and the poverty and the disease to gather in the Holy Land!

Itzik raised his hands and shushed the delirious throng, his face turned serious. "But if you do not repent of each and every transgression, you'll be relegated to the lowest level of Hell, for God has given me the power to know all the sins that every Jew in the world has ever committed." He pointed with one finger to his skull to indicate that all this information was crammed into his king-sized head, then he asked a man sitting in the first row. "You, Baruch the butcher, stand up and confess."

"I have sinned O Holy One. I have not said my morning prayers every day. I missed a prayer three years ago and again last month when my wife gave birth to our sons." He sat down with a solemn face.

"That's all of your abominations? You're sure about that?" asked the Messiah with a slightly mocking tone.

"Yes Messiah, that's all, except for the time that I ate a few slices of ham when I was starving during the famine six years ago. The Gentile butcher, Kowalchuk, was kind enough to give my family sustenance that day." The crowd nodded in sympathy; they knew all about hunger during their miserable lives.

"And how about the horsemeat that you sell every week and pass off as kosher beef?" asked the Messiah. The congregation groaned audibly as they heard the awful news. The butcher's face turned red. There were hisses from the crowd.

"Where is Osip, the tailor?" the Messiah asked. Osip stood up. "I confess to overcharging my customers on the coats and dresses that I make, but only a few kopecks per item."

"And?" said the Messiah staring at him.

"And I beat my wife senseless on two occasions last year, but I can explain that," he offered lamely.

"Anyone else?" asked the Messiah. Then Berkovitch, Kahanovitch, and Yaakovitch stood up and confessed to their tales of cheating, stealing and smuggling. The congregation quieted, as the remainder of the attendees pondered their own misdeeds. A few people edged to the exits, and soon it became a stampede. It wasn't long before the synagogue was empty except for Itzik, Berenshtein and the three rabbis.

"A hopeful start, Messiah," said Rabbi Kitzes, trying to veil his disappointment. "They'll be rallies in Rabbi Schmelke's synagogue next week, and Rabbi Mendel's the following week. Berenshtein can drive you in the donkey cart."

"That's fine, but first I need for you three to confess," said Itzik. "The people should know of your wrongdoings." Kitzes thought about Alexandra, Schmelke thirsted for vodka, and Mendel contemplated his poker losses with his congregants' donations.

"You know, with Passover not far away, the Jews of my town will be busy baking matzos and cleaning breadcrumbs from their houses," said Rabbi Schmelke.

Rabbi Mendel nodded his head in agreement. "Yes, maybe a visit in a few months. In the meantime, the angel could procure you a dazzling robe and teach you to raise the dead with less emphasis on sinning."

"It's important that you holy men confess, to set an example and to demonstrate..." but before Itzik had finished his sentence, the rabbis had turned on their heels and hurried out.

⤶

Rabbi Kitzes lay in bed with Feiga that night. He couldn't sleep thinking about his sins, and if he couldn't sleep, he couldn't talk to the angel.

"What did you think of the Messiah's performance?" he asked innocently.

"The people disliked him, like a cocky rooster he was, with a pecking nose. Are you sure he's the one?" Feiga being Feiga, was brutally honest.

"Of course, the Angel Tzadkiel wouldn't invent him."

"What proof do you have that this apparition is really an angel or just the unconscious fantasy in a rabbi's brain?"

"Well, he knew that Itzik lived in Shpola."

"How do you know there aren't ten Itziks living there?"

"But Itzik knows about everyone's sins."

"Most of what he said has been rumored. How many times have I told you that Baruch Fleisher sells horsemeat or that the tailor is a wife beater?"

"Itzik will be going back to his shtetl tomorrow. Tonight, I'll get further instructions from Angel Tzadkiel."

"What if your angel doesn't appear tonight?"

"I guarantee he's coming tonight," said Rabbi Kitzes as he rolled over on his side.

⤳

But the angel didn't come, and he never appeared again, despite every bedtime ritual that the rabbi could invent: reading the week's Torah portion, lighting a candle in the window, even leaving out a bowl of boiled potatoes and sour cream in case the apparition was hungry. For a time, the rabbi woke up five times every night to sing a special prayer that he composed, a prayer for the Angel Tzadkiel to come back for just a chat, to explain what had gone wrong. Feiga tried to sleep on a cot in the kitchen, but his chanting and wailing and crying was still audible through the thin walls. Finally, she couldn't stand it any longer. She moved to Odessa to look after her gravely ill sister who lived for another fifteen years. With time, the episode of the Messiah ebbed in people's minds, but the rabbi never forgot his humiliation.

One day, around 1900, Rabbi Kitzes concluded that he wouldn't live much longer. Berenshtein hitched up King David's replacement, Shlomo, and they set out to look for the Messiah. By that time, they'd forgotten where his hut was located. They asked the townsfolk in Shpola about a fellow named Itzik who once owned a black dog and some goats. The people gave them three names that met that description, but none of them claimed to be the Messiah, now or in the past. On the way back, Berenshtein was more taciturn than usual, but Kitzes heard him mumble under his breath, *some men are fools.*

It wasn't long after, that poor Rabbi Kitzes was lying on his death bed. He couldn't breathe unless he raised his head on four pillows. He suffered from congestive heart failure, a common ailment related to high blood pressure and disease of the coronary arteries, but of course, the doctors in those days had no treatment for that.

Feiga came back to nurse him in his final days. The special chicken soup that she made for him was loaded with salt and only made his breathing worse. One morning, she came into his room with a soft look in her eyes. She sat on the edge of his bed and watched her husband fight for air.

"Chaim, I'm sorry."

"Sorry for what, for leaving me for fifteen years?" Even on his deathbed he was bitter.

"Yes, and for thinking bad thoughts about you for longer than that."

"And why was that?"

"Aleksandra."

"You knew all this time?"

"I didn't want to believe it at first, in fact, I denied it for years."

"What changed your mind?"

"The Messiah."

And with that, the rabbi breathed his last breath and visited with the Angel Tzadkiel in heaven.

My Circumcision:
An Autobiography

Jews are prolific writers, and there are thousands of memoirs concerning Bar Mitzvahs, weddings, and funerals, but despite exhaustive research, I have found no autobiographical account of the bris (the Jewish rite of circumcision), so I've decided to fill this obvious gap in Hebraic lore.

My peregrination through the birth canal was unremarkable. I proceeded to breathe after the obstetrician slapped my gluteus maximi, and I sucked immediately— no surprise there—while my soul settled comfortably into my body, arriving from parts unknown, but most probably from a rock or a boulder after it had served some time in Gehenna. There was a vague intimation that my soul had inhabited a sparrow, and before that a fish and perhaps a dinosaur, while it couldn't be ruled out that I received a spark of spirit from Rudolph Schindler who invented the gastroscope before the Nazis ran him out of Germany.

Everything seemed to be going well. My father appeared from the father's waiting room—they weren't present at the birthing in those days—and told me that he hoped that I would be a good Jewish boy. I was staring at a picture of Jesus in my room, and with nuns all over the place, I just assumed that I was a Christian, although being bald and a little sallow, I hadn't ruled out Buddhism. I was to be saddled with a five-thousand-year history of misfortunes, not to mention the guilt, and now my parents were discussing cutting some skin around my penis to acknowledge that I was a Jew.

The next day Dad returned with a list of prospective mohels (ritual circumcisers). He had narrowed it down to three men; there were no women in the business in those days. A local butcher, Lazar Fleshler, seemed to have the most experience and his references were excellent, but because of his expertise, he charged fifty dollars for the ritual which in those days was a lot of money, plus he was not a kosher butcher and my father worried that the job might be tainted if there was some pork remnants on the man's hands, even though that seemed unlikely. The second individual was Asher Goldgraber who owned a deli, and was somewhat of a chiseler. He insisted on a package deal which included the post-bris meal. The third fellow, Solomon Klutznick, was a novice in his twenties, but had just finished his apprenticeship with a famous mohel in Chicago. He was the cheapest of the lot, charging only twenty-five dollars while trying to build up his clientele. My parents went with Klutznick, ostensibly for his enthusiasm and modern training. Holy mohely!

They went with a greenhorn, endangering my phallus to save a few bucks.

Before the memorable event, a no-nonsense nurse in a starched white uniform—possibly Nurse Ratched's mother or older sister—gave me a bath with a vigorous soapy scrubbing of my private parts that would shortly be on display. She wheeled me to a small conference room where a throng of people had gathered, mostly relatives whom I had never met, but if I knew then what I know now about my family, I would have started crying immediately. They placed me in the lap of my grandfather, and next to the chair reserved for Elijah, which of course was empty. He's the same prophet who never shows up on Passover to drink his wine.

Klutznick arrived looking handsome in a new suit with a fedora perched on his head, a Jewish Frank Sinatra. He started the ceremony with the blessing over the wine, sprinkling some sacramental vino on my lips to get me drunk so I wouldn't feel the pain. To this day, I have an aversion to Manischewitz wine and much prefer a pinot noir or a cabernet. He put a little helmet on my penis and trimmed away the foreskin with a knife. I was tipsy from the wine, but still able to shriek at the top of my lungs as my father and grandfather congratulated the rookie slicer on a job well done. Afterwards, my relations did what most Jews do, and that was to eat: bagels, lox, and cream cheese, along with knishes supplied by my grandmother.

My bris was over. I took my place in line as a traditional Jew although I didn't start to complain until I was able to talk. I don't want to go into embarrassing detail about the function of the mohel's handiwork, but suffice it to say, I was able to produce two children and my aim at the toilet bowl has for the most part been on target. More recently, because of an enlarging prostate, my trips to the commode have multiplied, but this has given me more time to look down and marvel at Klutznick's masterpiece. I've attended both of my own grandsons' ordeals and discovered that the quirky custom of ritual circumcision has not changed. The only modification in protocol was the mohel's announcement at the beginning of the ceremony: he instructed all in attendance to turn off their smartphones.

Who by Sword and
Who by Beast?

D r. Marvin Fish had made it to his sixty-eighth year, and some days he thought that was more than enough. But he kidded himself; most people fear death, and Fish was no exception. He knew that he hadn't lived an exemplary life, but who did? Yet the longer he lived, the more things unraveled, until he was embarrassed to look himself in the mirror, laughing that he'd grown a scruffy grey beard for that very reason. Something of himself was gone, something had died inside, but goddammit he'd tried, even if the void that was there couldn't be filled with the excuses that he substituted for truth.

He'd lost interest in his medical practice and the art and science of the profession. The AMA called it burnout, and sent him weekly emails with vignettes about physicians who'd rekindled their passion for the job, but Fish wasn't interested in another doctor's goody-two-shoes story. He spent unproductive time at his desk, absently scrolling sport scores on his phone, checking stock quotations, or browsing *embarrassing wardrobe malfunctions*, never discovering the revealing picture of the buxom beauty on the first page, just a click-fest of ads.

After medical school and internship, Fish worked in emergency rooms in the Los Angeles area, enjoying the warm weather and the beaches and the girls. He was something in those days, with a thick mane of sandy hair and a dark tan, like a virile lion. He would still be surfing if he hadn't run into Marsha Gluckstein, an old acquaintance from high school, who was vacationing in Malibu. A brief fling turned into a marriage after she became pregnant with twins, and Fish hung out his shingle in Wawapeka NJ, so that Marsha could be near their parents.

It was six o'clock, and he still had another hour of patient phone calls. He'd seen his associate, an African American named Eugene Oliver, leave the building an hour before. The young man had been with him over a year and was seeing just nine patients a day. Fish couldn't carry him indefinitely with that light of a load, but it was hard to build a practice when the town was losing population faster than he was losing grey hairs on his head. He wanted more time off, but somebody had to put in a goddammed day's work, and when his old patients called, they wanted to see him, even if he had become abrupt and obdurate, rather than the baby-faced squirt who looked like he'd just graduated high school, and Fish suspected that he knew about the cash payments that he hid from the IRS.

Mrs. Delores Possamunger was the last patient of the day. A crotchety woman with a hundred complaints every other month, but she needed her *prescription* as she always said.

"Good afternoon, Delores."

"Hi Doc, it's good *evening*," she remarked sarcastically.

Fish opened her chart on his laptop. "I see your blood pressure's elevated today."

"Well, yours would be too, if you waited this long."

"So, are you taking your meds?"

"Sure, I am, when I can afford them. It's not so much the Lopressor, and the Lisinopril, it's the glaucoma drops, not to mention the Ozempic for my diabetes."

"And why are you here?" Fish studied his watch and stifled a yawn.

"You know why I'm here. It's the back, always the back, and the left shoulder when I lift my arm over my head and turn my neck to the right, and then there's those headaches when I sleep on my back, maybe it's the pillow, but if you had a husband like mine, you'd feel like your head was in a pressure cooker too, and my hips and knees are shot from running up and down the stairs, fetching for that crochety old man who smokes all day in bed. Thank the Lord we have separate bedrooms. He refuses to come see you 'cause he says you don't do him a bit of good."

"How many do you want?"

"I'll need sixty oxys to get us through the month." She paid the co-pay with a crumpled heap of one-dollar bills. He put the money in the tin box in a drawer of his desk and billed Medicare for an *extensive visit with a comprehensive history and complete physical examination.*

৶

Fish sat down to eat at seven-thirty that evening. Sandra put a bowl of onion soup in front of him, and he glared at the school of goldfish crackers floating on the dark surface. They'd been together for eight years after the twenty-five-year debacle with Marsha, but his relationship with Sandra had followed a similar pattern, a nagging, tetchy woman, looking for sympathy. She'd quit working because of arthritis in her hands, and nowadays she had trouble getting out of a chair or so she said. A red rash developed on her face that the thirteenth-century physician, Rogerius, had described as looking like the bite of a *lupus,* a wolf. Fish had never seen a wolf's bite, never mind a wolf, except on the National Geographic Channel, but he knew what a *tired bitch* looked like. It looked like Sandra. And why should he take her to a movie or a good restaurant, or even give her a pat on the back, when he needed someone energetic, vivacious, happy, and just dying to go to bed with him.

He slurped a sip of the soup. "The onions are bitter, is there anything else?"

"Stew-meat with boiled potatoes and carrots." She ladled some on a plate, and he ate.

"I can still taste the onions, you must have put them in with the carrots." He took a few more bites. "And this tastes like pork, goddamned unkosher pork. How many times have I told you, no pork on the High Holidays, and I meant it."

"How was your day, Marvin?" The therapist had told Sandra not to take the bait when he wanted to argue.

"It was hell. I don't know how much more I can take. Thank god, it's Yom Kippur. I'll be off tomorrow, and

Dr. Oliver, can put in a decent day's work." He'd been Sandra's idea, a black doctor to look like the practices' changing clientele.

"Is it too late for the evening service?"

"Too late Sandra. Too late for anything."

～

Fish was belching eggs and toast when they arrived at the synagogue the next morning. He'd quit fasting on Yom Kippur a few years ago, about the time Sandra developed lupus, and Mark left for Australia, the only child that meant anything to him after Joel died. Then Mark's twin sister, Dahlia, the most brilliant student that Wawapeka High School had ever seen, walked out of Barnard six months before her graduation, and Marsha wouldn't give him her cellphone number. Sure, he planned to yell and scream at Dahlia, but what would any parent do if their brilliant daughter quit college and was tramping the streets of New York City? And he'd paid for the whole goddamned thing.

The congregation began in unison, *"Hear O Israel the Lord is our god the Lord is one. You shall love your God with all your heart and with all your soul."*

Fish repeated the words like an automaton, "love God with all your heart and with all your soul." He grunted perversely, love God? More than a haul at the blackjack table, or a Yankee victory in the bottom of the tenth? More than winning the third flight of the Stoneybrook Country Club's annual golf tournament after hitting a solid five wood two feet from the flagstick?

He thought of his father, reciting his prayers every
morning, wearing his yarmulke, his phylacteries, and his
tallis. He dropped dead at fifty-five, after a life of salt and
sweets and unhealthy Jewish food. What did God do for
him? An immigrant speaking broken English, who sold
beer and cigarettes seven days a week at a convenience store.

He looked around the sanctuary and spotted Marsha
across the aisle staring blankly ahead. She was with her best
friends, Norman and Helen Goldberg. They hadn't spoken
a word to him since he and Marsha had split. Hey, he had
his side of the story too. Didn't they want to hear about
Mrs. Marsha Cold Fish? He finally caught her eye, and she
smiled ever so slightly, maybe she missed him, or maybe
she was thinking *thank god I'm not standing next to you.*
Why couldn't she have left Wawapeka after the divorce?
Left that crappy antique shop with three customers a day,
maybe five on Saturday and six on Sunday, only kept afloat
by his alimony payments. Why didn't she pack up and
move somewhere warm and sunny, so he wouldn't have to
witness that Mona Lisa smile? Some Mona Lisa, with a
knife in her underpants.

He thought about little Joel who'd died of leukemia
at age eight. One day he developed a fever and bruises
all over his body, and Fish knew it was bad. They tried
chemotherapy and a bone marrow transplant, even a trip to
St. Jude's Hospital for a second opinion. He was buried in
the Jewish cemetery where Marsha's parents had been laid
to rest. They'd bought plots next to their son. He had no
idea what Marsha had done with them after they'd split,
and he didn't care.

The congregation stood up and prayed, they sat down and prayed, they stood up, sat down, stood up and sat down. Rabbi Lenny came to the podium. The rotund rabbi with the curly red hair and crepe-soled shoes, wearing the traditional white robe of Yom Kippur, pushing up his wire-rimmed glasses that had slid down his sweaty nose. The faithful husband to his wife, Naomi, with three successful kids, Judith, a doctor at the Massachusetts General Hospital, Alan, in law school, and the youngest, Batya, entering the Jewish Theological Seminary in the fall. Sensitive Lenny, who cried for three days after he ran over a rabbit's nest in the backyard while mowing the lawn, and the humorous Lenny who stated that the New Jersey Devils were the only team that a rabbi couldn't root for. A pious, generous, scholarly man, maybe a little foolish, but loved by his congregants. That was his brother, Rabbi Lenny Fish.

Lenny unrolled the Torah to the correct place, so that Rabbi Greenberg, his assistant, could chant from the holy scroll. When he was done, Lenny dressed the scroll in its velvet cover, cradling it like a frail infant, a very old frail infant, and placed it back in the ark with its brothers. Fish noted that all the Torahs had been donated by wealthy members of the Beth Shalom Synagogue, probably hoping for a shot at heaven he surmised. Fish checked his watch and flipped to the end of the prayer book, only 20 pages left. Depending on the length of his brother's sermon, the service would be over in less than an hour.

The congregation read the next prayer in unison, the famous Unetaneh Tokef, which spelled out what might befall a Jew who wasn't written in the Book of Life. He'd heard it since he was eight years old, except for the time when he was in medical school, when he'd skipped Judaism altogether, and then after Joel passed. Did God even care what happened to a piss-poor Jew like himself, who attended synagogue once or twice a year with a Gentile woman? Sandra had started working in his office, just after his relationship with Marsha was falling apart, or maybe before, he couldn't remember. Sandra liked the services and Lenny's sermons, and she'd come to know the melodies and the prayers. She'd been a great little nurse with a great little body, maybe not the smartest, but great with the patients and great in bed.

On Rosh Hashanah it is inscribed,
And on Yom Kippur it is sealed.
How many shall pass away and how many shall be born,
Who shall live and who shall die,
Who shall reach the end of his days and who shall not,
Who shall perish by water and who by fire,

Fish sniggered at the archaic absurdity of the prayer. Their house in Wawapeka was far away from any significant body of water and the smoke alarms were fully functional. Of course, if he and Sandra ever took that cruise, she might have an accident on the outdoor pool deck and fall in the ocean, but he'd probably never do anything like that. He could leave her for good, but she knew about the cash drawer and the opioid prescriptions.

Who by sword and who by beast;
Who by hunger and who by thirst;

Medieval stuff, by *sword* and by *beast*, no dueling in the Fish family, and death by a rhinoceros horn was rare. Fish wasn't one for metaphors. He looked down at his expanding paunch, dying by hunger seemed unlikely, and he chuckled to himself.

Suddenly, this chuckle was interrupted by something or someone calling him, a voice but no words, calling him to a place where he wouldn't want to be, a space with such terror... he took his pulse. It was racing like a metronome on presto, a tachycardia as those in the medical profession called it.

Who shall be at rest and who tormented?

Fish wanted to get up, get some fresh air, go home, take a diazepam. Sandra tapped his shoulder, she looked concerned, she must have noticed the whiteness of his face, the dread in his eyes. He took some slow deep breaths, and with effort he stayed.

He thought of the meal that his mother once prepared after the Yom Kippur fast: the chicken soup, the blintzes, even the jaundiced rutabaga that he hated. And why couldn't Sandra put something decent on the table? They'd probably go out for a hamburger this evening, a goddamned hamburger on Yom Kippur!

The congregation began to recite the long list of sins that required apologies.

"And the sins which we have committed before you for hard-heartedness... For the sin which we have committed before you with immorality. For all these God, pardon us, forgive us, atone for us." In 1965, Fish brought a transistor radio to the synagogue—a wire ran inside his dress shirt to an earphone—to listen to the World Series, the LA Dodgers against the Minnesota Twins. The Yom Kippur game that the Jewish star, Sandy Koufax, refused to pitch on religious grounds. The Dodgers lost. Fish's dad never stopped talking about the pitcher's sacrifice, more holy than any burnt offering at the ancient Temple in Jerusalem. At that age, no kid thinks about immorality or sins, you don't worry about a guy coming after you wearing a hooded cloak and a double-edged axe on his shoulder.

"For the sin which we have committed before You by scoffing and evil talk.

He looked at Sandra. She'd pulled out a Kleenex and was wiping a tear rolling down her scarlet face. Always crying, was he that big a *momzer?* Here he was, maybe in the final year of his life, and saddled with a woman who couldn't stop blubbering, blubbering about who, about what? About where? About him? Maybe he wasn't the perfect companion, but maybe she didn't deserve him either. He couldn't afford to marry her—Marsha had cost him three million dollars including alimony for twenty years, and he was far too old to make that up.

And for the sin which we have committed before You by causeless hatred. For the sin which we have committed before You by embezzlement... For all these, God of pardon, pardon us, forgive us, atone for us.

He was sweating like a pig. The Being was close, close enough to swing the axe as a searing pain tore through his neck. He leapt from his chair and pushed through the row of congregants, past Harry and Ethel Silverblatt, over the shabby loafers of Bernie Hochman, culminating in a dive over big-breasted Leila Feigenbaum, knocking her prayer book to the floor. He reached the aisle, hustled to the exit, and vomited his bagel in the parking lot. He got in the car and drove home wiping his drool with an old Kleenex that he found in the glove compartment. Then he'd remembered that he'd left Sandra at the synagogue. Well, he wouldn't be around much longer, she'd get used to it.

⌒

A few days later, he was sitting with his brother in the rabbi's study.

"What happened Marvin?"

"I didn't feel well. I couldn't sit there."

"I've never seen anyone run out of the sanctuary the way you did. We've had congregants faint, or someone leaves with a coughing spell or an urgent call from nature. Most people exit politely or a relative helps them out, except for poor Morrie Goldfine who died of a heart attack. The EMT's did CPR right in front of me, but someone just taking off and running, that's never …

"Goddamn it, Lenny. You don't have to tell me what I did. You'd run too, if something was breathing down your neck. *Who by fire?* I want to know Lenny. Do us sinners burn in Hell, like pork ribs over an enormous fire?... And he comes every evening."

"In your dreams?"

"No, in the hypnagogic state, between wakefulness and sleep. He's wearing a black hoodie with those large amber eyes. He comes if I take an Ambien or not."

"Does he talk to you?"

"No, just stares." There was an uncomfortable pause.

"How's Naomi?" Marvin asked.

"Call her if you want to know, you have her number."

"That's long past, Lenny."

"So, what do you want from me?"

"You're a religious man, a devout man. You're faithful to your wife, a devoted father to three successful children, six wonderful grandchildren, and your ninety-six-year-old mother-in-law loves you more than her sons. You're satisfied living on a clergyman's salary in a three-bedroom bungalow that the synagogue bought for you thirty years ago. You drive a ten-year-old Toyota Camry, pay your taxes to the final penny, even check the little box on your tax return so you can donate three dollars to the crooked politicians, and you take a vacation to upstate New York every summer, doubling as the rabbi for a Jewish camp. You spend your days officiating at circumcisions, Bar Mitzvahs, weddings, and funerals, sanctifying the members of your congregation, living and dead, even the schmucks."

Lenny couldn't conceal the sour expression that came over his face. "So, what's that got to do with you?"

"I need you to pray for me, every day for the entire year. Get me back in the Book of Life and keep me out of Hell. That's all I ask, a daily prayer for your brother Marvin. Maybe God will listen to a pious man like you."

"And what will you do for yourself, that will make me want to pray every day for you?" Lenny forced a smile.

"I'll repent, I'll repent like no one has ever seen. I'll be a repenting machine, morning, noon, and night, the king of repenting. I'll quit the gambling, the meanness, the lying, the boasting, even the overeating. I'll be a loving companion for Sandra, I'll make up with Marsha, and I'll quit the live chats with the call girls. I'll reconnect with my kids. I'll stop defrauding the government, and no more opioid prescriptions. Keep him away from me, and give me another shot at The Book of Life this year."

Lenny forced out the words. "I'll do my best for you Marvin, after all you're my flesh and blood."

"That's great Lenny, great to hear. I owe you one."

"But let me tell you something."

"What?"

"Death doesn't work that way. *For man also knoweth not his time; as the fishes that are taken in an evil net, and as the birds that are caught in the snare.* I guess you don't read Ecclesiastes."

"I guess not."

"The Book of Life is only a symbol for your journey on this planet. You'll probably live to be ninety-five." The rabbi laughed and Marvin laughed with him. "But can I ask you to do one thing for me, Marvin?"

"What? Anything."

"Come every week to the Friday night service."

"For my pious brother, sure I'll do it, and I'll bring Sandra." Marvin came over to his brother and embraced him as tears found their way down his fleshy cheeks. Lenny stared straight ahead.

⤝

And so, he swore that he, Marvin Fish, would change his ways. But as he turned into his driveway, an email from Sandra beeped on his phone. She was at the airport, waiting to catch a plane back to her hometown in Alabama. She listed the reasons for her departure: his lack of empathy, his dishonesty, his belittling, his hatefulness, and his selfishness. There was more, but Fish hit DELETE before he came to the end. He felt some sadness that she'd left, but what the heck, things had been off the rails for a while, and she'd left on her own without giving him a chance at repentance. No one could fault him for that.

He texted Marsha to tell her the great news of his reconnection to God, and suggested they meet for coffee. She seemed happy for him and promised that they'd get together, maybe next month or the next, maybe when she wasn't so busy. He called Mark in Australia and left a message on his phone. He told him how much he loved him, and to call him anytime. Several weeks went by without a reply, but hey, the ball was in his court. He searched for Dahlia on the internet but couldn't find her. At his age, he wasn't adept with computer searches. He made a note to hire a private detective to find her.

He stopped demanding cash payments from the patients, and requested a credit card or a check. He told Mrs. Possamunger and her cohorts that he wouldn't fill any more prescriptions for oxycontin, and the calls to the bookies stopped except for the Super Bowl and March Madness. He informed Eugene that he'd be retiring soon, and he could buy the practice with payments over five years. A few months later, Eugene moved to the West Coast to work for a hospital system.

Fish went to the synagogue every Friday night. He recited the prayers, sang the songs, listened to his brother's sermons, and beseeched God to allow him time to make amends for his misdeeds, and he confronted the apparition one last time. "Hey, come and get me, come and get an honest, loving, man." The Being blinked, and his yellow fisheyes went dark.

⤶

One day, Sylvester Maraschino came calling. He was sitting in Fish's inner office when the doctor returned from hospital rounds. He had no idea who had let him in. "Marvin, we have a problem."

"Oh." Fish knew why he was there.

"It's about your debt."

"Oh."

"One hundred and twenty grand. We've carried you for three years and the Boss is getting impatient."

"Oh yeah?"

"You need to start paying, or he'll be having a chat with the Angel of Death, about you." He chuckled, as he relished Fish's brains spattered on a sidewalk, his dead body gyrating in a cement mixer.

"How do you know about him, the Angel of Death?" Fish's face turned a pasty color, a cold ice pick shot through his spine.

"He's on our team in Bayonne, hell of a guy." Sylvester laughed.

Fish began to pay on his debt. He had a run of luck in his sports betting and he supplemented that with cash from the office. He put the money in a canvas bag, and Sylvester picked it up every other week. He missed a few Sabbath services, and then a few more.

↜

He received a call from Lenny two weeks before Rosh Hashanah, the Jewish New Year. "Where've you been Marvin, I don't see you anymore."

"I've been working, working hard. I'm still repentant, still working on that, but it's hard when you've got the debts I've got, and the practice is kind of on its back after the kid left."

"How's the nerves, Marvin?"

"What nerves?"

"You know the anxiety when you're falling asleep, the hypnagogic state."

"It's been okay, no more visits. How about you?"

"Pretty good. I've been getting a lot of indigestion lately and some excess gas, but the Pepcid seems to help, but maybe I need to see a doctor."

"You need to get your cholesterol and your blood pressure checked, maybe someone to perform an upper scope on your esophagus, and a colonoscopy while they're in there, someone that's slick with the black snake." Marvin laughed.

"Like the snake in the grass, Marvin?"

"Are you still praying for me, Lenny?"

"Don't worry, I'm the king of praying for you, Marvin."

⌐

Three days later, the family gathered for the funeral in the little chapel off the main sanctuary. Naomi, Lenny's wife, was in the front row with their three wonderful kids. Marvin's sisters sat behind her, sniffling into copious Kleenexes. Marsha dabbed tears from her eyes. Sandra had flown in from Alabama and was sitting next to her. Dahlia sat on the other side of Marsha; she'd found solace at an evangelical church on Staten Island and was working as a waitress in a Japanese restaurant. Mark wasn't there, but he'd be coming back from Australia next week to spend time with his mother.

The assistant rabbi, Harold Greenberg, arrived to console the immediate family before the funeral began. Everyone huddled together to hear the rabbi's prayer, everyone except Marvin Fish, who sat disconsolately in the back of the small room mourning his brother, Rabbi Leonard Fish, who had died in his sleep.

Five Minutes Left on the Clock

It seemed an unusually tranquil morning on my back porch. As I slowly settled into my rocking chair, being careful not to spill the cup of artificially sweetened coffee on my Kindle or my polyester golf pants, I couldn't help but notice an ashen cloud hovering overhead, and just then, a little bird chirped a tuneless song. I took a deep breath, and the fruity scent of an unnative honeysuckle species assailed my nostrils.

Simply, a cisgender white man, sitting on the deck of a well-appointed house on an affluent block of the comfortable suburb of Creve Coeur, Missouri. The city's name, translated from the French, means *broken heart*, as in a broken-hearted Indian princess who committed suicide by jumping into the lake of the same name when she couldn't swim. A retired, old-mannish Jewish physician, a cowardly candyass, ensconced in a deep plush cushion on a faux bamboo chair whose legs rested on a surface of composite floor boards made from nylon and peanut shells.

But the serenity was not as it seemed, for the Covid, one of God's creatures, had arrived on our blighted planet;

a microorganism that had developed the ability to enter our nasal passages and find its way to our lungs, then spend some days trying to destroy its human host, succeeding in 3% of those infected, particularly older persons like me. Millions had been infected and thousands had died, while the jobs of those that lived disappeared like the butterflies in my backyard after the invasive honeysuckle overran the milkweed.

We all wore masks and washed our hands and kept six feet apart from other homo sapiens, at least in Creve Coeur we did, a little patch of unfamiliar blue in a red state. And because of overwhelming angst and depression, we had the same urge as the Indian princess, to jump into the same lake with cement blocks attached to our ankles. The source of our agitated melancholy was a potpourri of existential threats and tragedies: our health and that of our loved ones, the unlucky victims of the Covid, dwindling finances, the lies of a crazed president, conspiracy theories, George Floyd's murder, the unfed, the oppressed, the sweltering planet, even the viability of our country and maybe civilization, everything at the same time. That's what the shrinks call free-floating anxiety, the worried mind—mind as well worry about everything. And let's face it, at my age, death is a foregone conclusion, if not yet a reality.

That very morning, before camping out on my unwood deck, I'd watched cable television document the frightening increase in the number of coronavirus deaths, followed by video clips of Mr. Floyd asphyxiating from a policeman's knee to his windpipe, followed by protests in the streets of every large city, followed by footage of our orange-faced leader marching past the tear-gassed throng to the Episcopal church, holding a Christian Bible upside down, a holy book given to him by his daughter who had converted to Judaism. Maybe she didn't need it anymore.

I'd turned off the television and left for the outdoors as an act of mercy to myself, but it was too late. A sense of foreboding arose in my solar plexus and moved up to my chest like a cobra responding to a snake charmer's flute. Nausea engulfed me, and my heart left its regular beat for a samba. I experienced a vertiginous spin of the head, like the earth had rotated a bit off its axis, or conversely, I had rotated a little off *my* axis. I closed my eyes and took deep breaths in and out, in and out, as my yoga teacher had instructed before the class had been suspended due to Covid.

"Well, how dee do, Max." I opened my eyes. A large crow had perched on the railing of the deck. This wasn't the little bird that had chirped incoherently, I was pretty sure of that. There was an odor of sweat and urine and stale peanuts that one might experience at a zoo of some kind.

"Your voice, do I know you? Your voice—it sounds so much like—"

"Duddy, your neighbor from long ago."

"Duddy Silvermintz? You're Duddy Silvermintz?"

"I'm dead now, Max. Dead and I've returned to being a bird after my time in Hell, only six months this time. I keep hoping that someday I'll reside in Paradise."

"No hurricanes or wild fires or crazies in that neck of the woods, I guess." There was a tinge of sarcasm in my voice.

"We need to be pious and righteous to go up and not down, and of course, we need to love God and believe in Him. You *do* believe in God?" I felt him staring at me with both eyes at once.

"I do, in a…a metaphorical or maybe a metaphysical sense, I guess."

"Then you're not certain."

"I'd feel more confident if He talked to me after getting my attention with a burning bush, or some freshly baked bread from the firmament. You know, a small miracle or two for the huddled masses." I laughed.

The black fowl bobbed his head apprehensively. "Remember Howard Stein?"

"Sure, he lived on our block. He was a druggie, a delinquent and later a thief. Never finished high school, but he loved Mama's brownies, and she liked him too. He'd loan you his baseball glove or his brand-new bike with the brakes on the handlebars, if you just asked. He flunked the seventh grade, and then after his dad passed away, he got with the wrong crowd and became addicted to heroin. I couldn't sleep for a week when I found out that he died of AIDS."

"His soul lives on in a paving stone at the end of the Leibowitz drive way. He's inhabited the same piece of granite for twenty-five years and probably has a couple of epochs remaining." He paused and cocked his head toward one shoulder. "God sends me to talk to people just before—before—"

"Before what?"

"Before they die."

"You came here to tell me that?"

"Someone had to, no more grim-reaper stuff, just a raven without a hood. It's less intimidating."

"And when will that be?" I felt the tightness in my chest, maybe the coronary arteries were gasping for oxygen before the heart quit forever.

"Soon," he answered.

"How soon?"

"Soon."

"From Covid?"

"Could be cancer, and you're at the age for a stroke, the kidneys might go kaput, and of course the old ticker isn't—"

"And the Paradise that you mentioned?"

"Not so much for you right now." The bird cawed hoarsely.

"Not so much right now?"

"Let me explain. After someone dies, his soul could fall in a lake to be eaten by a fish, and that fish to be eaten by a religious person. If the proper blessing is said, that soul could ascend to the Garden of Eden. Similarly, if it lands in a wheat field and is subsequently made into a loaf of bread, then have the luck to be eaten after a blessing, or possibly find its way to a blade of grass and get eaten by a heifer just before a kosher slaughter—or better still—"

"But what about souls that go directly to the Promised Land, just straight up?"

"You didn't qualify for that Max, but don't feel bad, not many of us make it there that way. It's like playing in the major leagues right out of high school."

"So, it's a bit about luck, maybe fate, you never know what might happen, but unlikely."

"Something like that."

"Come to think of it, I'd be delighted to reside in the Garden, to partake of the delicious fruit, the mangos, the cantaloupes and the sweetest pineapples, while staying far from the Tree of Knowledge. I'd befriend the angels, sing the psalms, and talk philosophy with Maimonides, maybe hike the trails with Moses once in a millennium."

"Something to look forward to in its proper time." The bird flapped his wings like he wanted to fly away.

"But why not me? I lived life the best I could. I treated many patients and saved many lives and didn't bill the uninsured. I was a good husband, okay maybe not a great husband, maybe not much in the sweet-nothings-in-the-ear category, or the holding-hands-in-the-movie-theater category, or the peck-on-the-cheek-before-going to-the-grocery-store category, but a good husband. My children and grandchildren have an interest in my well-being, and I've given my share to charity, I could give more if it will make a difference."

"No, it won't make a difference Max. Look at your Jewish soul and where it's been."

"What do you mean?"

"The people who hosted your soul over the years, like your ancestor who thought he was Abraham from the Bible."

"Rabbi Avrum Plonk, my great-great-great-great grandfather?"

"He dreamt that God ordered him to sacrifice his son, Issur, your great-great-great-grandfather. He took the poor boy to the top of a hillcrest, then waited for the words of God which never came. His frantic wife divorced him, and poor Issur never recovered from such an ordeal."

"What about my relatives in Poland and Russia and Hungry and Romania, people that I never met?"

"The Holocaust?" The bird cocked his to the side and stood on one leg.

"Did God punish the Jewish people for their sins, or was He impotent against Hitler, or did we Jews become better people for that horrendous experience?"

"That's always been a stumper."

"That's the explanation for the Holocaust? A stumper?"

"You got a better one?" The bird self-consciously pecked at the ersatz-cedar railing. "Remember the seder when you were ten years old, 1958 I believe, the whole family was there."

"I remember, it was the year that I got tipsy from the Manischewitz wine. We ate some matzo ball soup that included a boiled chicken that may have been past its prime, and I might have complained. For the main course, we had a delicious brisket, heavenly potatoes, carrots, asparagus, a kugel or two, but I demanded corn on the cob. Corn was forbidden to be eaten on Passover then, and so was rice, but now the rabbis have changed their minds—"

"You argued with everyone, Max, you were drunk."

"I was upset that the Egyptians had to perish in the sea. They were just soldiers taking orders from the Pharaoh, and still mourning the deaths of their first born. And if God could split the Red Sea, why couldn't He knock the hell out of Hitler or Nebuchadnezzar or Titus for that matter?"

"You failed the test of faith, Max."

"I'm going to Hell because of some disputes at a seder."

"And your attendance at the High Holiday services—"

"I attended until I was twenty-five."

"You brought your transistor radio to the synagogue and listened to the World Series with a wire through your dress shirt connected to an earpiece, just like Norman Fish."

"Maybe my soul was praying with my brain turned off?" Duddy rustled his feathers in disapproval.

"And when you spread that story about a dinosaur named Ruthie who ate the forbidden fruit in the Garden, and God got angry and expunged the dinosaurs from the Bible. That's blasphemy Max, pure and simple." Duddy tucked his head under a wing.

"That was a joke, a stupid joke." I felt a swirl in the head and some thumps in the thorax. My voice cracked, and I thought of taking a Xanax, if I could get to the medicine cabinet on legs of jelly.

"As a matter of fact, none of your ancestors have ever lived in Paradise," remarked the bird. "None of them made the grade."

"But how do I even know that such a destination exists?" My natural skepticism resurfaced.

"You must have faith in God's presence, Max. He imbues all living things."

"I guess when there's only five minutes left on the clock—just before the buzzer—everyone wants to believe that there's a *there* there. Even an atheist wouldn't turn down a place in the Garden, would he?"

"That would be unlikely."

"But my gosh, I have a damn good soul, most of the time. I'd bet on it. I honestly would." My eyes pleaded. My voice begged.

"Death isn't always fair," confided the bird. He opened his beak a crack, which is as close as ravens get to a smile. "Hey, you could transmigrate into a bird. There are worse things than that, like being a lizard or a frog, and it's unlikely you'll be a rock, I'm pretty confident of that." Duddy flapped his wings. "And don't forget the piety, that would help too." Then he flew away.

I closed my eyes and listened for the tiny sparrow, but all I heard was the rattle of a failing air conditioner unit and the persistent buzz of a weed eater. Soon I was dreaming of the Garden of Eden, sitting in a peaceful mossy place by an unpolluted brook, and I was eating the sweetest pineapple that anyone ever ate; I even offered up a slice to God before eternity set in.